SUGAR GUARDS

SUGAR DADDIES #16

CHARITY PARKERSON

--Warning: This book is intended for readers over the age of 18.

Copyright © 2019 Charity Parkerson
Editor: BZ Hercules & Consultants
ISBN: 978-1-946099-57-0

❀ Created with Vellum

INTRODUCTION

Yaro and Pytor have been a couple for as long as they have memories. Legend has no one. The longtime couple are about to change that.

Since cancer stole Legend's mom, he has been completely alone in the world. He has never considered himself smart or talented in any way. His looks and ability to charm anyone have kept him from ending up homeless by working as an escort. Everyone is willing to hire Legend as arm candy, but no one wants him for him. Each time Legend meets someone he is truly interested in dating, they are already in love with someone else. Pytor and Yaro are no exception. At least, that's what he thinks.

Pytor and Yaro have always been together. Neither man can recall a time without the other. Not once have they considered sharing their lives with anyone else. Until they meet Legend, that is. Legend is beautiful and sweet. He's an old soul who needs a place to rest. Yaro and Pytor want to give him the home he desperately needs, but Legend is a little harder to convince than they expected.

After a botched attempt at making things work, the longtime couple will have to prove they aren't like everyone else Legend has met in the past. That's a tall order, considering Legend has every intention of completely disappearing from their lives.

ONE

Henry: *Painting an image for you... the two of us in Vegas. Champagne, dancing, and **mumbles** boring charity dinners. Ignore that last part. It's this weekend. Short notice, I know. However, I'll double your fee.*

Legend: *Hey, gorgeous. You know how much I love Vegas. What's the cause?*

Henry: *Kids, dogs, the homeless. Cancer, veterans, the elderly. I have no idea, angel. Pick the one that convinces you to join me so I'm not stuck rotting in the corner.*

Legend: *I'm always available to save some dogs. Send me the details and I'll be there. I can't wait to see you.*

IT WASN'T DOGS. FUNNILY ENOUGH, THE CHARITY for the weekend event was for animals. Legend never paid much attention to the reason for these events. Double his usual fee of three thousand a night for an entire weekend was more than he could pass up.

Growing up, Legend had thought about becoming a cop. That seemed a respectable profession. He doubted anyone grew up with dreams of becoming an escort. The money was better, though. Plus, he had ADHD and hadn't done well in school. He didn't have what it took to go to a job every day. That was the tip of the iceberg as to how he had ended up here. Nonetheless, Legend liked his work, for the most part. He chose his clients. Sometimes, he came across men who treated him like a whore, even though he didn't have sex for money. They saw paying his high fee as rights to do whatever they liked. Those were the ones he never saw again. But clients like Henry made those occasional asses worthwhile. Henry was rich, sweet, and generous. At fifty-two, he wasn't too old to find someone he didn't have to pay. Legend wasn't sure why he didn't try. Not that Legend was complaining. He liked Henry's company. As long as the man wanted Legend to join him at events, he would.

Henry wasn't the reason Legend now regretted taking this job. They were in Vegas. Hundreds of miles from home. Yet, the two men who lived in Legend's head and under his skin were there too, stroking him with heated glances every time Legend looked their way.

Three months ago, Legend had been invited to Pytor and Yaro Volkov's home for a day of parkour-style play at their indoor ninja warrior course. The place had waterfall hazards and rock formations along with metal rings and jump points. It was badass and appealed to Legend's adventurous inner kid on every level. The day had turned to night before becoming morning, slipping away like seconds rather than hours. They had talked almost the entire time about everything and nothing. Legend swore the pair were nonstop flirts, even though they were married to each other. Legend was a shameless person, but he had blushed more times in that one night than he had in years. When the morning came, guilt and realization set in. They belonged to each other. The longing that grew in his chest was as ridiculous as it was useless. He always wanted what he couldn't have. Legend had left with the intention

3

of never coming back. He had gone back at least three days a week since. Those visits were becoming every bit as painful as the days he didn't see them. That was why he had decided—once and for all—to stop. Now they were here, testing his resolve again.

"At least he seems to spend his ill-gotten gains on good causes."

Legend's gaze jumped to Henry at Henry's statement. It took him a moment to work through the claim. He had been staring at Pytor and Yaro again. They were Zander Kapra's bodyguards. Henry must have thought Legend had been watching Zander as he moved from table to table while making his rounds. Legend smiled, hoping to look as innocent as possible. "I don't know what you mean."

Henry glanced Zander's way and back again, as if debating whether he should corrupt Legend with the knowledge that Zander's money was mafia money. Even though he had never met Zander, Legend already knew about his illegal ties. He just kind of wanted to see what Henry would say. Legend had never heard Henry speak badly of anyone. "It doesn't matter," Henry finally said, brushing the unpleasantness away. "Just promise me you'll never accept a job from that man."

"I don't date married men."

Henry's gaze sharpened. "Do you know Zander?"

"He's wearing a wedding ring," Legend said, explaining away his knowledge of Zander's life. "It's a personal policy of mine to never date anyone married. I'm also not shopping for clients. I'm sorry if I gave you that impression. That man in the bright green jacket with no shirt underneath looks familiar to me. I was trying to figure out where I've seen him."

Henry didn't bother looking. It wasn't like the shirtless man sitting with Zander could be missed. He stood out like a crystal chandelier hanging from a garage ceiling. "That's Wyld West. He's eccentric, to say the least, but when you're the third richest man in the world, you can afford to be whatever you like."

A light switch flipped in Legend's head. He hadn't truly been trying to place the man. Pytor and Yaro held all his thoughts, but Legend recognized Wyld's name. "Didn't we attend some charity event of his? For the homeless or something?"

Henry smiled. It was a bright and happy-looking gesture. He was obviously relieved Legend hadn't been pining for someone else but thinking about a date they had been on together in the past. "Yes. Last year. I forget sometimes how long we've been attending these events together. You must get tired of never being taken on a real date."

Legend blinked at the off-hand remark. He wasn't sure how to take it. "No one wants to date me."

For a moment, Henry stared at him in open confusion, making Legend realize he had taken the statement wrong. Finally, Henry shook his head. "I meant by me. It seems like I only ask you to attend events. I don't think I've ever simply taken you out for a night on the town. You should get to go to a nice dinner." Henry snapped his fingers. A bright smile stretched his lips. "The opera."

"Oh." Legend had nothing else. Part of him wanted to be mortified for accidentally admitting he wasn't a catch. The rest of Legend wanted the last five minutes back. His confession had nothing to do with confidence. Legend owned a mirror and liked to think he was a good person. No one worth having would ever date him while he entertained other men for money. He had learned long ago that he had to choose—this job or a life. For now, he chose his job. Legend tore his gaze away from Henry and went back to checking out the room. He didn't like it when people caught glimpses of his soul. It made him feel empty.

White tablecloths, flowers, and candles topped every surface. Every guest was dressed to impress. The food had been bland and the liquor strong. Legend tried thinking about anything and everything to keep his gaze from sliding back Yaro and Pytor's way.

"I wonder sometimes why you accept a lowly six grand for two nights when you could be under an exclusive contract with me for much more." Legend's gaze swung Henry's way and didn't budge. Henry had never talked like this before. "If you were to choose only me, I would take very good care of you." Henry took his hand. His light brown stare never wavered from Legend. "You'd never want for anything in my employ."

Legend could see the honesty in Henry's eyes, but this wasn't what he wanted. An image of the two men he couldn't shake flashed through Legend's mind. They were a fantasy he couldn't stop hoping to achieve. On the other hand, what he wanted was an impossible dream. They were married... to each other. Legend meant nothing. "You're asking a lot," Legend said, dodging. "I would be giving up an entire client list for one person who might decide they're sick of me in six months. Then what? I would be out of work and homeless."

Henry's mouth lifted in one corner. "You could marry me instead, then you would be set for life."

Legend couldn't breathe. His natural charm kicked in, saving him. "What would all your other men think? They'd be heartbroken. I'd find my tires slashed every other day."

Henry didn't smile as Legend hoped. "I'm one hundred percent serious, Legend. Think about it, okay? Now." He stood, keeping ahold of Legend's hand. "Take one last walk with me through the garden and I'll let you go be young with all the gorgeous men who keep flashing me jealous looks."

Legend pushed to his feet. He let Henry pull him close as they headed for the closest set of French doors, leading out into the hotels' private garden area. "It's me they're shooting envious looks. They all wish they were on the arm of the most handsome man here."

A soft laugh caressed his ears as they stepped outside, and the warm night air washed over them. "You have no idea how much I wish I could have back my youth. When I was your age, times were very different. I couldn't openly be with someone like you back when I looked good enough to actually win someone as beautiful as you." He flashed Legend a smile. "You wouldn't know what hit you. I would've swept you off your feet."

"You already blow everyone else away. Rewinding the clock wouldn't change anything."

Henry squeezed his arm. "I wish time was as kind as you are."

With Henry holding his arm, they wound their way through the hedges and flowers until they found a cement bench. "Would you like to sit?"

Henry turned his face toward the full moon. "No. It's a beautiful night, but I think I'll go to bed and end the night on a pleasant note." He dropped his chin and met Legend's stare. "You know I don't pay you to spend time with me because of your looks, right? I genuinely care about you."

He didn't know how to respond. Usually, Henry deposited money into Legend's account and they never openly spoke about it. This was the second time tonight Henry had mentioned it. Henry seemed sad—like maybe spending time with Legend made him lonelier than being alone. Legend went with his gut. He kissed him. It wasn't a romantic kiss. He didn't intend for it to be. Money aside, they were friends, and he liked Henry. This would likely be the last time Henry hired him. He had gotten too close. That happened with some clients. If he didn't accept

Henry's offer to either be his exclusively or marry him, then Henry wouldn't contact him again.

"I promise I'll think about your offer," Legend said, pulling away. He would. Legend wasn't just saying the words. He had been for sale all of his adult life. One day, he would be in Henry's shoes, looking back at his youth and wondering why he hadn't tried harder to be happy. The thing was, Legend didn't believe in love. Maybe that wasn't strictly true. He didn't believe he was the type of person who could be loved. There were dozens of couples he could name that seemed to genuinely love each other. Legend had people who had cared about him over the years. People like Henry. No one had ever loved him. Legend had been fond of several men. He hadn't met anyone he couldn't live without. Legend fought against the whisper in the back of his mind, telling him that wasn't true. There were two men...

Henry brought Legend's hand to his mouth and pressed a kiss to Legend's knuckles. "Goodnight, sweetheart."

"Goodnight."

Legend watched Henry walk away. He always had a hint of sadness in the back of his mind, waiting to overwhelm him. Sometimes, Legend had to work harder than others to keep the depression at bay. He didn't want to go inside, so he sat and stared at the sky. Legend didn't know what to do. Normally, he wouldn't think about Henry's offer at all, but Legend was tired. He spent a lot of time trying to make other people smile, hoping he might feel a hint of the happiness he gave away. Henry was a good man. Legend didn't give a fuck about the age difference. Henry would be good to him. Maybe a nice, quiet life was exactly what he needed. After all, Henry knew exactly who Legend was, but he still wanted him. It was something to think about for sure.

"Are you hiding from us?"

Legend smiled at the sound of Pytor's voice before turning his head. Yaro and Pytor headed his way. Legend's heart squeezed in his chest. They were so big. Legend could picture himself between them. Warm. Protected. Aroused.

"Is it possible to hide from you?"

"No," Pytor and Yaro said in unison.

Legend's smile grew. They were beautiful. Expensive suits, one set of sweet brown eyes, and a set mismatched eyes—one green and the other blue. Pytor was taller by a few inches, but they were both wide-shouldered mountain of men with dark hair. Each had silver strands threading their hair, making them look distinguished. Yaro's voice was softer and his accent thicker while Pytor's voice was deep and Legend could imagine it rumbling against his skin. Together, they made it hard to breathe.

"I'm hiding from the crowd."

"You can stand between us and we will keep you safe," Yaro offered.

"As good as I am at being in the middle, aren't you supposed to be guarding Zander?" Legend heard himself. He was incapable of not flirting with them. They brought something out in him.

Both men's eyes danced with laughter, but Pytor was the one who responded. "Zander has gone to his room for the night. We are free to please you."

"That'll be two minutes of your lives you'll never get back. What would you two like to do after that?" Legend couldn't stop smiling. His face ached with happiness.

"Two minutes," Yaro scoffed. "How deprived you've been. But we have another way to spoil you. In-room gambling. We will make you lots of money."

Legend curled his nose. "In-room gambling? Is that a thing?"

"Of course," Pytor answered. "It's a channel on your TV. You control your betting with your remote. It's only for high rollers. They give you a code when you check in. We are very good. Yaro and I will pay.

12

You keep the winnings. What do you say? Wanna take us back to your room for some late-night fun?"

They had no idea. "Sure. The three of us. Alone. My room. Playing. Sounds amazing." Damn, it did, even though Legend knew things would never go where he wanted. This was why he tried staying away. It was hell wanting Pytor and Yaro. The longing was gut-wrenching. Never in his life had Legend been so sure of his own mind. The deep pit of need inside him had nothing to fill it. This entire crazy mess had moved into a place of being painful to him. Being with them hurt. Legend wasn't sure he could handle much more. Legend massaged his chest as he stood. "I'm on the third floor." Even he heard the unhappiness in his voice. Legend tried changing his tune. "What floor do they have you on?"

The pair eyed him, as if trying to decipher his earlier tone. Legend kept a smile in place by force of will. Finally, Pytor shook his head—like shaking off his confusion. "The seventh. Your room is closer."

Since Legend couldn't get a read on Pytor's bland tone, he led the way inside and to the elevator. He swore he could feel the heat radiating from their bodies as they waited. Legend tried breathing through his mouth, hoping not to catch their scent. It took every ounce of his strength not to bend at the waist and suck air. The way he felt; it was powerful. Then the door slid open. Pytor set his hand on the small of Legend's back and Legend knew it was him by his touch alone. The moment nearly hobbled him, because Legend recognized how deep he had let things get.

On the short ride to the third floor, the men—somehow—managed to stand even closer. Legend kept catching himself closing his eyes, taking in their warmth.

By the time the elevator set them free, Legend no longer wanted to move away. "I almost hate we haven't passed anyone along the way. I didn't get to make anyone jealous that I'm taking the two hottest men here to my room."

"We could go back and make the trip again," Pytor suggested, his voice full of laughter. "We were cheated too. No one got to whisper behind their hands about us, wondering how we convinced you to take us upstairs."

A chuckle escaped Legend. His cheeks ached, making him realize how big his smile had become. They made him happy in a way no one else did. Legend couldn't explain it. They were more than friends. Friends didn't feel like this. A nervous flutter mixed with anticipation hit as he let them inside his room. It was like he could feel their hunger. Legend knew it wasn't all in his head or wishful thinking. Something grew between them. It got a little bigger every day.

He took off his jacket and tossed it onto the chair by the door. His tie came next. He undid the top two buttons on his shirt as he made his way to the bed. "So how does this work?" Legend glanced over his shoulder. He was nearly blasted off his feet at the combined heat in Pytor and Yaro's stare.

Yaro shook his head.

Pytor smiled as if coming to his senses. "Use the TV remote." The pair joined him as he sat on the end of the bed, flanking him on either side.

Legend powered on the TV and played with the remote, determined to ignore the growing tension. He found the games. Pytor relieved him of the remote and entered his high roller information and private code.

"We will pay any losses," Yaro explained. "Your winnings will settle when you check out. We are good luck. You'll see."

Legend already saw. He had never felt luckier. Pytor showed him how to make bets. It was way too simple. He could easily see people losing their asses.

Legend tried keeping his bets small. He didn't want to cost the guys anything.

Pytor scoffed. "You are playing kiddie games. Let me bet."

Legend handed over the remote and tried not to blanch as Pytor entered a number that almost made Legend throw up a little in his mouth. He couldn't repay that. Yet Pytor smiled as he passed back the remote.

"Hold on," Yaro said, saving Legend from begging them not to make him do this. "You need the good luck." They leaned forward and gave each other a nod. Before Legend could guess at their intentions, they squished him between them, and each kissed a cheek. Legend's heart raced the moment their lips met his skin. It was over as fast as it happened. "There. Now you bet."

With shock rendering him mute, Legend followed Yaro's order and hit the button. He won. "Holy shit."

The men laughed and kissed his cheeks again. "Go."

At Pytor's order, Legend played again. He won. Excitement had him forgetting his discomfort. He never won more than a few dollars at a time. This one game had him up by tens of thousands. "I can't believe it. You two really are good luck. I never win anything." He hit the button again, and he lost, cutting his winnings in half. "Damn. I forgot to wait on your lucky kisses. I'm still up, though." He cast a laughing gaze their way. They were both smiling and sitting even closer than he remembered.

"You're not the only one," Yaro said, laughing.

Legend snorted at the innuendo. "I think I should stop while I'm ahead. If I lose your money, I'll never forgive myself."

"One more play," Pytor demanded.

Yaro nodded. "One more." Yaro's tone was so playful, Legend couldn't resist them. "This time, we make sure everyone has all the luck."

Yaro kissed the corner of Legend's mouth before leaning across him and kissing Pytor. Legend couldn't stop smiling. He loved being with them. They were so happy. It was beautiful. Being with Yaro and Pytor filled Legend with something he couldn't describe. They were his best friends. He loved them.

Pytor laughed and kissed the corner of Legend's mouth before quickly moving away. Then Yaro kissed the other corner and didn't move. The air changed. Legend held his breath. Pytor pressed his lips to Legend's cheek. He didn't move either.

Legend's mind was blank. He couldn't think or breathe. Yaro's hand landed on Legend's knee. Legend's lips parted on a pant, transforming their kiss. Without a thought, he tasted Yaro and then Pytor. There was no tongue involved. No one tried to deepen the kiss. Legend had never been more scared to think. Yaro's hand slid higher. Legend's heart beat so hard and fast, it was the only sound he could hear. Not once had he ever been nervous over a kiss. Never before had he wanted anything as badly. As one, Yaro and Pytor swiped from Legend's thighs to his chest—like they'd choreographed the move, pressing him backward onto his back. Legend was so damn hard he couldn't move. Their lips brushed Legend's cheeks before moving back to his mouth. Their kiss turned into a three-way kiss he had never experienced. No one deepened their kiss. It was an equal act. No one dominated, but he definitely felt overwhelmed. It was just a brushing of slightly parted lips that had Legend ready to come in his pants.

Yaro pulled away first. "You won, sexy. Now you can sleep in peace."

He didn't recall playing.

"Goodnight, gorgeous baby," Pytor whispered against his lips.

"*Spokoynoi nochi*," Yaro added as they each rolled from the bed, leaving Legend panting and staring at their retreating backs.

He swiped his hands up his face. It seemed he had made more of things than he should have. Again. Legend cleared his throat, trying not to sound as turned on as he was. "Goodnight." His chest and throat hurt. Pytor and Yaro were married. He was just their friend. They would never want him the way he wanted them. It seemed there was a cultural difference in which they kissed their friends in a way he wasn't accustomed to handling from friends. This was Legend's lot in life. He wanted people who didn't want him. The funny thing was, it wasn't like he saw people didn't want him and then he decided he had to have them. Legend just seemed to pick out men who ultimately didn't see him as more than a friend. Of course, he hadn't meant to want Pytor and Yaro at all. His heart was greedy. Legend crossed his arms over his chest. He wouldn't see them again after this weekend. That was the best thing for his heart. Legend didn't know how long he stared at the ceiling after the pair left. His body needed time to cool. It wasn't happening. Legend couldn't stop feeling their lips against his skin. He swore he could still smell their cologne.

A growl slipped from him. Legend rolled from the bed. "Fuck everything." He angrily unbuttoned his shirt before tossing it aside. Maybe he could refund Henry half his fee and go home. Legend didn't know if he could handle seeing Pytor and Yaro at tomorrow's scheduled events. He was so goddamn tired of everything. Most of all, he was sick of being him. Legend unbuttoned his pants and whipped off his belt, tossing it toward his shirt. Someone knocked on the door. Legend didn't bother buttoning his pants. If one of the guys had forgotten something, they would just have to deal with his state of undress.

Legend yanked open the door with more force than necessary. His brain froze. "Henry?" He tried reeling back his surprise. "Is everything okay?"

Henry's gaze dropped to Legend's bare chest before sliding lower to Legend's unbuttoned pants. His gaze snapped back to Legend's face. "I'm sorry. If you have company, I can wait until the morning. I realize you're no longer on the clock."

Legend realized he probably still looked tousled and horny. He opened the door wider so Henry could see he was alone. "Well, if I'm no longer on the clock." Legend snagged Henry's hand and hauled him inside the room. Henry wanted Legend for

Legend. No one else could say that. He headed for the bed with Henry in tow. "What did you need, sweetie?"

"Oh, um." Henry sounded embarrassed and shy. It was sweet. "I couldn't sleep."

"I can help with that," Legend said, maneuvering Henry onto the bed.

Henry sat. He looked ready to bolt. "Um."

A smile that felt wicked even to him pulled at Legend's lips. He liked this version of Henry. He looked human and reachable in his white t-shirt and plaid pajama pants. Legend straddled Henry's lap, keeping his weight braced on his knees. He toppled Henry over onto his back. Henry's hands landed on Legend's thighs. Even though he looked nervous, Henry's cheeks were flushed. He couldn't hide that he was turned on. "You can tell me no," Legend said as he braced himself on his palms and slowly lowered his head.

Henry shook his head. "No. I can't."

Legend kissed him, hoping to hide his smirk. It was empowering to be wanted. He had been rejected a lot lately. First by Adrik, and then by Yaro and Pytor. Legend needed someone to make him feel like he wasn't completely alone. He was so used to being used and nothing more than arm candy that he didn't even feel human some days. Legend was just going through the motions of living while trying to make everyone else happy. Maybe that was all this was too. Legend didn't know if he could tell the difference any longer.

It took some coaxing to get Henry to relax. Then his hands swept up Legend's sides. Their kiss turned heated. Legend let Pytor and Yaro go. They weren't his. They would never be his, but Henry could be. Legend needed to start facing reality. Henry was real.

———

Yaro chewed his bottom lip and tugged down the covers on the bed. Pytor could feel the man's worry like a tangible thing. It had the muscles in his shoulders bunching. For as long as he had memories, Yaro had been his entire world. He couldn't let his baby stay upset.

"We did the right thing."

Yaro's sexy mismatched gaze slid his way. "Did we?"

Pytor set one knee on the bed and crawled toward Yaro, nodding. "He needs time to think. We are overwhelming."

"This is true," Yaro said, visibly relaxing. He pulled a pained face that mimicked Pytor's feelings. "He was very sad tonight. Why is he always so sad?"

While fighting the urge to rub his chest, Pytor snagged Yaro around the middle and hauled him into bed. "He didn't push us away or toss us out. That's a good sign, I'm thinking."

Yaro pushed, toppling Pytor onto his back before straddling his hips. "This is also true. I just hate waiting. You know I am not the patient one."

The lingering hunger from the kiss they shared with Legend grew as he stared up at his ridiculously sexy husband. The love he felt for Yaro never lessened. In fact, every year it got bigger. "It's a lucky thing you have me to use as you please while we wait for Legend to come to us. Tell me how I can entertain you."

A wicked glint entered Yaro's eyes. His sexy mismatched gaze moved down Pytor's body. "Hmmm. I can think of too many things. Where should I start?"

Pytor linked his fingers behind his head and waited. He would give Yaro anything.

"Damn," Yaro whispered, looking at Pytor like his next meal. "You are beautiful. I will never understand how I got so lucky."

Pride swelled Pytor's chest. "We are not lucky." He could never let Yaro believe that. They had survived too much together. Fought too hard to stay at each other's side through the years. "You should kiss me. My lips miss yours."

Yaro braced his weight on his palms and lowered his head. His lips lightly brushed Pytor's mouth. Love washed over Pytor like a tsunami. "I would never let your lips be lonely."

Their tongues met and brushed. Pytor never grew tired of the sensation of Yaro's body against his. He didn't know if other people felt such a powerful pull to their other half, but Pytor did. He rolled, tucking Yaro beneath him and deepening their kiss. Yaro chuckled—like he had known Pytor wouldn't stay passive long. Yaro shoved Pytor's underwear down, freeing his erection. All thought left Pytor. Nothing mattered but the love of his life and the way they set each other free.

TWO

The faintest hint of sunlight peeked through the sheer curtains covering the two windows that met in the corner of his room. Outside, the Vegas outline met his stare. Legend blinked at the sight. It always took him a moment to gather his bearings when he traveled. Memories of the previous night flooded Legend's brain. Legend immediately locked down his emotions. He couldn't let himself have those things. Feelings always wrecked him.

Legend rolled. Henry was gone. Legend stared at the large expanse of empty bed at his side. With his thoughts and emotions behind a wall, Legend sat up and reached for the papers stacked on the bed where Henry should be. The handful of words scratched out on the hotel scratchpad didn't ease the tension building in his shoulders.

Decided to go home. Here's your plane ticket—H.

Sure enough, his plane ticket home was tucked beneath the scratchpad. Legend settled back against the mountain of pillows. He wished he was surprised. Legend couldn't stop staring at the plane ticket. Part of him wanted to laugh at his stupidity. Why had he thought Henry was any different than hundreds of other men who tried wining and dining him over the years? If he hadn't been so upset about Yaro and Pytor when he had opened the door to Henry last night, Legend might have seen Henry's ploy for what it was—the same bullshit on a different day. Henry had talked about marriage, saving Legend, and then left just long enough to let him imagine what that might be like. He had shown up a few hours later, hoping Legend had time to get excited about the idea so he could easily slip inside Legend's bed before disappearing from his life. It was a game. He had been played. In this case, it hadn't been dreams of a lavish and respectable life that had tricked Legend. Legend had played himself with dreams of two men who would never want him. Either way, he was everyone's fool—as usual.

Legend snagged his cellphone and called the

number on the back of the ticket. It rang three times and immediately put him on hold. He stared at nothing, doing his damnedest to keep his mind blank. Hopefully, he could convince the airline to let him have an earlier flight. If not, he would call every single airline until he got a flight in the next few hours or he would rent a car and drive home. Either way, he was done with this place. Maybe he was just done.

YARO HAD A SICK FEELING IN HIS GUT. THE sensation had kept him tossing and turning all night. As much as he wanted to believe they had made the right choice by leaving Legend alone last night, something felt wrong. By the time they rounded up Zander and Maverick so they could join the day's events, Yaro had chewed off his nails and had a headache from clenching his jaw.

The instant they joined the crowd, Yaro's gaze ate up the room, searching. Their blond Adonis was nowhere to be seen. The man always stood out in a crowd. Normally, all they had to do was follow everyone else's stare and there was Legend. Not today. He wasn't there. His gaze shot to Pytor.

They shared a silent conversation. Something was wrong.

Pytor touched his lips to the shell of Yaro's ear. "I will put out the feelers."

With a subtle nod, Yaro went back to searching while still keeping Zander blocked from all the people. Zander's safety was Yaro's responsibility. He would never shirk that, even though his desperation screamed Legend was more important. Yaro snapped to attention as he heard Pytor ask about Henry.

"What happened to Henry Krill? I thought he was here last night."

Everyone knew of Henry Krill, whether they knew him personally not. He was old money from a respected family. His family owned a well-known chain of banks around the country. Henry was the sole heir. His pockets were deep, his reach long, and he obviously had his sights set on Legend. He was also nowhere to be seen.

The middle-aged man, who was as wide as he was tall, smiled kindly at Pytor's question. "I heard he left in the middle of the night. Lucky bastard. The rest of us are stuck." He let out a hearty laugh, obviously unaware of the cuts he opened with his words. "That young fellow he had with him left about two hours ago. I saw him getting in a cab. Not sure what happened there. I've never seen Henry let the boy out of his sight."

Yaro breathed slowly through his nose, trying to squash him temper. Something had happened after they left—they had either caused a problem between Henry and Legend by being in Legend's room while he was working for Henry, or Legend had run from them. Neither scenario set well with Yaro. In fact, both ideas left him feeling hollow. First off, no one treated Legend like property. He was no man's personal slave. Secondly, Legend had no reason to fear them. Third, goddamn it all. He was beyond reason. Yaro listened with half an ear as Pytor thanked the man for the info. He didn't perk up again until Pytor went after Zander.

"Hey, boss. I heard a rumor that some people were simply writing big checks and leaving. We should do the same."

Zander eyed Pytor with open interest. "Really?"

Yaro jumped in, backing his husband. "Yes. I just heard the same. It seems there are some ridiculous games planned for this evening. Since people are not wanting to make fools of themselves for charity, they are giving their monies now."

Zander rolled his eyes. "I wondered why Krill had left. Why do the uber rich always want you to do stupid shit and give them your money? We are too old for three-legged races and bunny hop. Dear God. I will slip someone my check now so we can go home. Fuck all that noise. I miss my bed anyhow."

The moment Zander turned his back, Yaro flashed his brilliant husband a smile. They would be home before the end of the day, and then they would go get their man. They had let this game play on too long. It was well past the time they should have claimed Legend as theirs.

CONSIDERING HOW MANY TIMES LEGEND trailed from one room to the next, Legend couldn't believe his legs didn't hurt. Even for someone who loved the gym, it was an impressive workout. Legend checked the app on his phone that tracked steps. He had walked nine miles. Some of that had been through two airports, and the hotel, but still. Even knowing he was wearing a hole in the floor, Legend couldn't stop. On the other side of stopping were his thoughts. Legend couldn't do that. Not today. Maybe tomorrow he could handle life again. Today, Legend was one wrong thought away from driving his car off a cliff. Instead, Legend walked and created a checklist in his head. First, he needed to ditch his work phone and dismantle his website. Once he disappeared from the scene, he could slip away from his life. There was nothing keeping him here but Adrik. Since Adrik lived with Yaro and Pytor, Legend needed to accept they wouldn't talk again.

Damn. Legend rubbed his chest. That hurt. He finally stopped pacing and stared into space. Could he leave this town and everything he knew behind? Legend shook his head, shaking off the doubt. He didn't have a choice. Something had to change for him and it was past the time he should have moved along. He no longer had what it took to stay on this path. Maybe the spark for life it took to do this job would return someday. Until then, he needed to try his hand at something else.

With his decision officially made, Legend moved to his bedroom and found a clean pair of workout shorts. As he took a shower and went through his nightly routine, getting ready for bed, Legend's mind still shied away from the heaviest of his burdens. He refused to acknowledge that he might be running. It wasn't like it mattered anyhow. No one in California would miss him.

The doorbell chimed as Legend pulled back the blankets on his bed. Legend froze. No one visited him. The bell cut through the air again and Legend grabbed his phone. He pulled up his front porch camera. Pytor and Yaro waited. The way Yaro sat half perched on Legend's porch railing screamed they would wait all night. Legend scrubbed his fingers through his hair. His gaze shot around the room, looking for anything to save him. Nothing came to mind. With nothing left for it, he headed for the living room. Legend took a deep breath before pulling open the door.

"Did we do something to scare you away?" Yaro asked, stepping inside without waiting for an invitation.

He was unprepared. There was no time to think. He hadn't expected them to show up and question him, especially tonight when they should have still been in Vegas. "No." Legend turned his face away as he made the claim and closed the door behind the pair.

Yaro's voice turned sad. "I see. We did do something wrong."

Legend's gaze jumped to Yaro. He couldn't let them believe that. "No." Even he heard the honesty behind that one word.

"I see," Pytor said, mirroring Yaro's earlier words. "We've given you the impression that we're toying with you." The pair exchanged a lingering glance. With a sharp nod, they peeled off their shirts. Their hands went for their jeans.

Legend's mouth went dry. His brain glitched at the sight of their perfect bare chests. "I don't understand what's happening here." Legend couldn't stop the desperation in his voice. They had shown up with no warning and now they were stripping. He couldn't think.

Pytor's voice turned hard. "Yes, you do."

Legend matched his tone. "No. I don't. You're married, and I'm—" Legend snapped his teeth together, damn near biting off his tongue, because he didn't know how to finish that. He wasn't married. He couldn't be the thing that destroyed them. Legend's heart couldn't take them touching him if they didn't mean it. Everyone used him. If they did, he might not survive it.

"'Take a breath, angel. It's our job to take care of you now. You don't have to be sad anymore." Yaro's sweet tone mixed with confidence and had Legend's walls slipping. He wanted to believe.

"Don't give me hope." Even to his ears, Legend sounded like he choked on air. There had always been a small voice in the back of his mind, saying they would end up here. He had been adamantly telling himself it wasn't true, because he couldn't handle another damn loss right now.

Yaro closed the distance between them. Legend's brain screamed he should run now while he had the chance. Yaro's eyes looked so damn sincere. "Don't take away our hope." Before Legend could fully process everything, Yaro kissed him. Legend felt flayed in two. His brain shut down and his heart took over. Legend held Yaro's face between his hands while Yaro tugged at the strings of his workout shorts. They loosened at Legend's waist. An overly warm body pressed against his back. Teeth sank into his shoulder. Legend gasped around Yaro's tongue. The way they had overwhelmed him last night was nothing. The pair completely wiped his mind.

Yaro gripped his jaw and pushed his face away before turning his head toward Pytor. Pytor captured his mouth. Before Legend could acclimate to Pytor's rough kiss, his dick was in Yaro's mouth. Legend's knees buckled. Only Pytor's strong arms kept him upright. He tried to hang on to sanity between the erotic way Pytor kissed like a fucking god and the massive talent dancing on his dick. Legend liked to think he had stamina, but he was not going to make it long. He writhed and moaned. Need owned him.

There were two men here he needed to please, and Legend was about to end their night in Yaro's mouth.

Pytor chuckled against his lips. "Yaro is very good. He will make everything better and then you will take us to bed."

Legend wanted to nod. They were definitely going to bed together. He didn't have control of any part of his body. Every muscle seized as Yaro sucked, licked, and squeezed. The room went dark at the edges of Legend's vision. Oxygen disappeared. Yaro sucked Legend's crown with the perfect pressure and an orgasm tore through him, ripping a cry from his lips. His entire body shook. He had no control. They didn't give him time to recover.

Pytor swept him off his feet. "Where's your bedroom, angel?"

"Down the hall. It's the only room with the light on." Legend's house was nice and in a great neighborhood, but it wasn't huge. He didn't doubt Pytor's ability to find his bedroom.

They were there and Pytor eased him down onto the bed in a flash. Legend was still blinking and trying to figure out what happened to his life. Pytor glanced around the room. "This is nice. Which of these bedside tables has the goods?"

Legend pointed toward the one on the left.

Yaro headed for it while Pytor stripped. After Yaro dug through the drawer and tossed a few things on the bed, he peeled off the rest of his clothes. Now nothing stood between any of them and Legend couldn't stop staring. The men were perfect. They were huge and sexy. Legend was a tall guy and he worked out all the time, and still he felt small. A sudden need to earn this overcame him.

"Damn. You two need to get in this bed. I've got plans."

Both sides of the bed dipped as they did as told. Gorgeous chuckles rumbled around him, but Yaro was who responded. "Oh, sexy. We have plans too. You have no idea how many ideas we have discussed in the past few months. We will make you happy."

Legend's heart melted at the words. He couldn't explain his reaction. Yaro's words sounded like a promise—like this was about way more than one night together. As they joined him, Legend realized he didn't know where he wanted to start. He wanted them equally. Thankfully, they seemed to know. Their mouths came for his lips. That perfect three-way kiss was upon him again, except this time, they deepened it. Legend hadn't known this was possible. If he was being honest, he had been to bed with more than one partner at a time before. In fact, he had been to bed with three men before. This was different. This wasn't a night of overly aroused fun. He cared about Pytor and Yaro. Truthfully, he loved them. They were closer to him than anyone. He wanted this night to go on forever.

Legend rubbed and massaged every place he could reach. Pytor rolled him onto his side, leaving him for Yaro to kiss while he kissed Legend's spine. Legend found himself moving lower. His tongue, lips, and teeth explored Yaro's body while lubed fingers toyed with his ass. He was every bit as hot as he had been before getting blown. Legend was beyond ready for more. He wanted everything. With no real plan in mind, Legend ended up on his knees between Yaro's thighs, licking and sucking the man's dick. He rubbed and massaged, playing with Yaro's ass as Pytor did the same to him. Then something much larger probed at his ass and Legend wanted it. A moan rumbled in his throat as he pressed backward, begging for more. Yaro's cock slipped down Legend's throat as Pytor's dick filled his ass and time slipped away. Reality disappeared. He was nothing but heart and desire. Every fantasy he had pleasured himself to in the past few months came to life. He was in between the two people who meant everything to him. They moved together and strained together, reaching for a new height as one. Legend's cock pumped out pre-cum all over the bed like a second orgasm. He had never been more aroused in his life. Words were gasped and moaned around him. Legend couldn't hear a thing except for his heartbeat. His body burned. His heart overflowed. This was what he had been waiting for his entire life. Legend felt... whole. He felt Yaro tense beneath him.

"Jesus, angel. You're fucking amazing. I'm about to blow."

Pytor growled behind him. The sound nearly caused his knees to go out. "Your sexy asshole is sucking me dry. Goddamn."

Between their praise and the way Pytor's dick kept punching that button, a second orgasm hit with no warning. He sucked hard on Yaro's dick while cum pumped from his cock. Salty fluid filled his mouth. Cries bounced from the walls.

"Goddamn," Pytor gasped. His grip tightened to the point of bruising on his hips. He thrust deep and hard. Legend couldn't breathe. He swallowed as fast as he could while his mind scattered to the wind. Pytor collapsed, rolling to the side at the last moment so he wouldn't crush anyone. The three of them gasped, sounding like they had finished a marathon together. Legend found himself squashed between two sweaty men. Their arms wrapped around him. Their hearts beating against his skin. He was home and safe. Legend felt loved. His eyes burned. He didn't want this to ever stop.

Pytor couldn't stop watching Legend and Yaro sleep. There was so much pride in his chest, he could barely breathe. These were his men. He had been waiting months to have them here—in one bed and resting peacefully. Legend was tired. Soul weary. No one could look at him and not see it. Yaro and Pytor had been in his shoes, living a life that did not fit but incapable of leaving. Being a prisoner of fate was a nightmare. They could give Legend a new life. A peaceful existence.

A smile tugged at Pytor's lips as he took turns covering his men, pulling the blankets higher. Yaro's hand found his in his sleep, the way it did every night. This time, for the first time, their fingers linked on Legend's stomach. Pytor took a breath. They felt right. He had zero doubts. They were three pieces of the same puzzle, clicking together perfectly. There hadn't been an ounce of awkwardness or anything between Yaro and him when it came to Legend. They had immediately started flirting with zero jealousy. Then, one day, Yaro had looked over at him. They had spent a moment staring into each other's eyes, nodded, and said, "He belongs with us" at the same exact time. They had always been on the same page like that. For as long as Pytor could remember, it had been like they could read each other's minds. Finding Legend was no different.

"We will make you happy," Pytor whispered. He didn't want to wake Legend, but he needed the vow out there. Yaro and he knew themselves and this was meant to be. They would cherish Legend as they did each other for as long as he allowed.

THREE

Cloud nine looked damn good to Legend.
He hadn't stopped floating on air all day. Pytor and
Yaro had woken him with breakfast in bed before
taking turns kissing him goodbye. As much as
Legend hated to watch them go, they had to work.
They had also made him promise to present himself
at their house at exactly six when their boss was
finished with his schedule for the day.

Finding ways to entertain himself while too
excited to breathe properly was interesting. He had
gone to the gym, to visit Adrik at the casino—secretly
hoping to see his men with no luck—and he had even
gone shopping. Legend couldn't recall the last time
he had bought anything for himself that wasn't
completely necessary. He didn't much care for

shopping, but Legend needed a way to fill the day. Several times, Legend stopped himself from buying something for Yaro and Pytor. The last thing he wanted was to look crazy. There was a good possibility he was insane, but he didn't have to show it.

The craziest part of the entire situation was that Legend would have expected himself to overthink. To question every tiny detail. Instead, he felt like everything was okay for the first time in years. He wasn't worried that it had been a onetime thing and now Yaro and Pytor wouldn't want anything else to do with him. Legend had felt the way they cared about him. This wasn't for the fun of it. Nor was it scratching an itch. They were going somewhere. Maybe he didn't totally know where yet, but he wasn't worried or in a hurry. For once, Legend just wanted to be happy.

After trying so hard to fill his day, Legend ended up being ten minutes late. He knew, as he navigated the driveway of the multimillion-dollar home, that Yaro and Pytor would already know he was there. Security was intense at the home of Zander Kapra. Zander owned all the Luna hotels and casinos on the west coast as well as Vegas. It was also rumored he was a mafia boss, which was true, but whatever.

Legend had never even seen the guy. The house was so fucking massive, it was hard for two people to cross paths unless intended. Plus, it seemed, for the most part, Zander and his husband stayed to one side of the place while Yaro and Pytor had their space. Pytor said Zander didn't want them to feel like they were on duty twenty-four-seven. This was their home. In fact, Legend always parked and entered near a door that led straight to their living room. They hadn't made him knock in ages, since security always knew the moment anyone was on the property and they always expected him. Tonight was no different. Legend let himself inside.

The living room was dark except for the light of the TV. That was enough to show the outline of his men cuddling on the huge leather couch. The smell of popcorn filled the air. They glanced his way as he came through the door. Both men wore sweet smiles that had Legend's heart melting. They started to move apart. Legend waved for them to stop. "You don't have to do that for me."

They didn't listen. Pytor motioned for him to sit between them. "No. We have missed you and want to cuddle."

It wasn't like he could argue with that. Legend slipped into the spot between them and immediately found himself engulfed in men. They took turns kissing him while they both held him. Legend's insides danced with happiness. It was amazing how much he had missed them in the short few hours they had been apart. He had spent so much time pining after the pair. Now that he had them, Legend couldn't get enough.

"Have you eaten?" Yaro's question brushed against Legend's neck, causing goosebumps to rise on his skin.

Legend fought a pant. "No. It smells like you've been having a movie and popcorn kind of day."

Pytor chuckled against the shell of Legend's ear before his tongue traced it. Legend was already hard. "That was Adrik and Yaro. It was his reward for a good day of studies."

"Oh." Legend didn't have anything brighter with Pytor and Yaro each massaging a thigh and moving higher. Adrik lived here too—somewhere in a distant part of the huge dwelling. Legend had steered clear of any talk of Pytor and Yaro when he had visited Adrik earlier at the casino. Truthfully, as innocent as Adrik was, Legend wasn't sure how to broach this topic. It was equally possible they were a secret. Legend's chest ached at the thought.

"Did you miss us?"

"Always." The confession came out sounding breathless as Yaro moved lower, kissing his collarbone.

"We wish to take you out and show you off," Pytor said, immediately wiping away the fear his own over-thinking caused. "But first, you are too tempting to ignore."

"Mhmm. Agreed," Yaro growled, massaging Legend's erection through his jeans.

Legend wasn't a passive lover. He had allowed them to render him useless last night. Legend couldn't let that happen every time. He buried his fingers in Yaro's hair and tugged, forcing Yaro to meet his gaze. "I hope you have condoms and lube in here, because I'm about to fuck you."

Yaro's lips parted on a gasp. He looked enthralled. Legend's hunger doubled. He felt powerful with such a mountain of a man at his mercy.

Pytor leapt to his feet. "I will hunt and gather."

Legend's hungry gaze watched Pytor as he headed down the hall. Even though, logically, Legend knew both men were way older than him, they didn't look it. Only the streaks of gray in their hair gave them away. Their bodies were too hard to show any wear from time. If they had any imperfections, Legend's heart made him blind to them. Only when Pytor disappeared from sight did Legend manage to tear his eyes away. His gaze returned to Yaro. He wore an unbuttoned dress shirt and dress pants. His rock-hard abs were on display. He had so many lickable parts that Legend didn't know where to begin.

"You're so goddamn sexy," Legend growled, incapable of stopping the words. He captured Yaro's mouth with more force than intended. Legend pushed and tugged at Yaro's clothes, needing him nude. Yaro tried to help while also tearing at Legend's clothes. They parted only in short bursts until there wasn't a stitch of clothing left between them.

Pytor reappeared. "Damn. Look at you two." The lust tinting his words made Legend's dick twitch. Legend found himself rubbing against Yaro, giving Pytor a show. He wanted the heat in Pytor's stare. Legend wanted to see that fire snap. His body still felt Pytor from last night. He wanted it again. Legend needed that huge cock, making him hurt with pleasure.

Pytor handed him a condom. His eyes hardened. "Put this on. Let me watch."

Legend made a show of rolling the condom down

his length while both men eyed him in open hunger. He had never felt more powerful.

Pytor handed him the lube next. "Oil Yaro's asshole."

Yaro melted to the floor and dutifully presented his asshole for lubing. Legend slipped to his knees. He couldn't resist the sexiness of Yaro's vulnerability. His trust was too beautiful. Legend squirted some lube onto his fingers, but that wasn't enough to satisfy his heart. Without giving Yaro time to deny him, Legend went in face first and tongued Yaro's ass. The sound he made had an evil laugh rising in Legend's throat. He speared Yaro with his tongue, wetting his asshole, and giving him a preview of what he would soon do with his dick. With Yaro panting, Legend replaced his tongue with his fingers. He wasn't merciful. Legend popped two fingers inside Yaro and curled upward to massage. Yaro slapped both hands on the floor and strained against Legend's fingers—like he fought for more. He didn't want to look away, but Pytor buried his fingers in Legend's hair and tugged his head back. His mouth covered Legend's. Pytor's kiss was hard and bruising—like punishment. Legend's cock leaked.

"Fuck him," Pytor growled against his lips. "He's begging for your dick."

Legend didn't need to be told twice. The moment Pytor set him free, Legend fell on Yaro, impaling him. Yaro immediately transformed into a wildcat. He short fingernails tore at Legend's skin. He bit and fought, trying to get even closer—like he wanted to rip his way inside Legend. Legend had never experienced anything like it. He worried he wouldn't last long with Yaro fucking with his head. Legend pounded at Yaro's ass. His every thought was focused on nothing but the sensation of being inside Yaro. He had one goal—release.

Then, Pytor was there. His palm flattened between Legend's shoulder blades, holding him in place. Legend was buried to the hilt inside Yaro. He couldn't move. Pytor was too strong. Pytor's large fingers probed at Legend's ass. Legend dropped his head to Yaro's chest and fought for air. He was no longer in control. Pytor changed their angles. His huge cock forced its way inside Legend's asshole, stretching him well beyond comfort. He rocked forward, burying himself deep and shoving Legend even deeper inside Yaro with the force of his thrust. Legend's eyes tried rolling back in his head. Oxygen meant nothing. In fact, nothing mattered at all but the ecstasy his body endured. He was useless. Pytor was the one in charge. Legend was no more than a tool as Pytor took control. He held Legend in place and thrust, using Legend to fuck Yaro even as he plowed away at Legend's asshole. All Legend could do was hold on. He clung to Yaro and got fucked. There was no other way to describe what happened to his body. Sweat slickened their skin. With his mouth open, and Pytor taking bites out of his back, Legend fought for air around his cries. His body rocked with no help from him. Pressure crawled up his shaft while Pytor's cock massaged at the perfect angle internally.

"This ass is mine," Pytor said, pounding harder. "Say it's mine."

"It's yours." The words came out rasped and barely audible. Legend was incapable of more.

"We will fuck you in ways you've only dreamed of," Pytor promised. "Every night. One of us will be in this ass, making you beg. So, always come here ready to get fucked. You belong to us now, Legend." Legend felt it. He knew he was theirs.

"Oh my god. You're so goddamn good," Yaro cried beneath him. "I can't hold it." A cry sounded beneath him. Hot cum pumped between them. Yaro's asshole clamped down on his cock, then Yaro's ass sucked, and Legend was lost. Pulse after pulse rocked him. He swore he went blind in one eye as an orgasm tore through his body. All he could do was shake and fill the condom with jet after jet. Pytor was still in control. Legend was a helpless mess of moans and shaking. Pytor didn't slow. He didn't let up. Legend's dick was still getting thrust into Yaro while Pytor took no mercy on his ass. The pleasure was almost painful. The lower half of his body was trapped between his men. The mewling noises Yaro made and the growled promises of sexual torture Pytor made held Legend's brain captive. He was their willing hostage. Legend didn't want to ever stop. Every fantasy he had ever had about them didn't hold a candle to reality. They were like heroin. It had only taken one trip to get him addicted. Now, after a second dose, Legend was certain he would die if they ever decided they didn't want him. He clung harder to Yaro. Love filled his chest. They were his. He would kill to keep them.

EACH TIME YARO CAUGHT SOMEONE STARING, more pride filled his chest. He knew he was with the two hottest men there. Sweat rolled down his back as he moved to the music. With his back against Yaro's chest and ass grinding Yaro's crotch, Legend held the back of Yaro's neck and pulled Pytor closer. Pytor dipped his chin and brushed his lips across Legend's before doing the same to Yaro. Legend turned his head and joined in. Yaro could barely breathe around the happiness choking him.

They were regulars at the club inside Luna Hotel. Since their boss owned the place, everyone knew them. This was the first time anyone had seen them with Legend. For Pytor and Yaro, this was a declaration. Not only were they unashamed, everyone needed to see Legend's face and understand he belonged to them. They were security for the west coast mafia boss. Openly declaring they would kill anyone who messed with Legend wasn't only beating their chests. They would literally kill anyone who disrespected Legend. He was theirs.

The music slowed. Legend turned where he could hold them both. Pytor shuffled even closer. The pressure in Yaro's chest increased as they moved at the same time and pressed their foreheads together as they swayed to the beat. Yaro had always loved Pytor so much, he could barely contain it. Legend made them more. He was in so deep, his love had surpassed happiness to become terrifying. There was such a thing as too blessed. He worried this would disappear and he would be wrecked past the point of repair. The fear had Yaro holding his men a little tighter. He would do whatever it took to keep this.

The slow song ended, and Legend leaned away smiling. He tugged at his shirt, like he tried to get a breeze. "I need a drink."

Pytor nodded. "Agreed."

As one, they headed for the bar. Legend ordered a water, making Yaro realize he had never seen the man drink alcohol. "Do you not drink?"

Legend winked as he turned up his water. He chugged half the glass before answering, "I like being in control too much."

A hum rumbled in Yaro's throat. He liked being controlled. Pytor handed Yaro a glass of straight vodka. Yaro sipped before he admitted all his kinks in a club, surrounded on all sides.

A knowing smile touched Legend's sexy lips. His wicked gaze never wavered from Yaro.

Pytor draped his arm over Yaro's shoulders and pressed his lips to Yaro's temple. "When you finish your drink, we'll go find something to eat."

Yaro nodded, but he couldn't look away from Legend. There was only one thing he wanted... technically, there were only two people he wanted. Neither was on a plate in any restaurant. Unless the pair were up for getting arrested for lewd acts tonight.

Legend dug out his wallet and pulled out a bill. Yaro swallowed his irritation as Legend tried getting the bartender's attention. When he finally got the man to look his way, the guy eyed the bill and shook his head. A line appeared between Legend's brows. He looked their way as he shoved the money in his front pocket. "I've never had a bartender refuse a tip before."

Yaro kept his smile as innocent as possible. They would break that man's legs if he took money from Legend. Pytor would ensure a hefty tip was left at the bar, but Legend's money was no good here. He was part of their family now.

FOUR

For several long minutes, Legend stared at Yaro and Pytor, who were sleeping like gigantic bears. They both snored. Not annoyingly so. Just low grumbles—like huge animals, putting off too much heat and sucking in more than their fair share of air. Legend smiled at the picture they made. He rubbed his chest. Life had been so empty before them. Now he had two men who took up too much space. Thank god they had a huge bed.

It took some doing, but after some wiggling and slow crawling, Legend managed to slip from between his men without waking anyone. Following a quick trip to the bathroom, he headed for the kitchen. Pytor had gotten the drop on him last time. Legend wanted to make breakfast for them. While Legend had made a lot of money working as an escort, he didn't have much to show for it beyond a nice car and house. It had cost him almost everything, helping his mom while she battled cancer. Legend had to stop and take a breath. Sometimes grief sucker-punched him at the oddest moments. Legend blinked back the tears. He didn't know if he would ever be whole again.

Legend shoved the hurt to the back of his mind. He opened the fridge and concentrated on making breakfast. Pytor and Yaro might wake up any minute. He didn't want to lose this chance to do something nice for them. Legend almost made it. As he loaded plates onto a wooden tray, a solid chest collided with his back.

"What are you doing?"

Legend jumped in his surprise at Pytor's appearance. For someone so big, he moved ridiculously quiet. Legend turned, smiling. "Go back to bed. I made breakfast this time."

Pytor didn't smile. He eyed the tray, looking downright disgruntled. Without a word, he took the tray from Legend, set it aside, and started removing plates. "Yaro is allergic to these things," he said, getting rid of the eggs and wheat toast. He kissed

Legend's cheek. "Go to bed. I will bring things we can eat."

Legend didn't move. He wasn't one to get his feelings hurt easily, but something about this hit him hard. Eggs and toast didn't take a ton of work. It was the point, he supposed. It was like his gesture was unappreciated. Legend didn't have anything to offer the pair. They already had everything, including each other.

"Sorry. I didn't know about the allergies." Even he heard the defeat in his voice.

Pytor hauled him forward. He cupped Legend's face and kissed him deep, leaving him breathless despite his hurt feelings. "Your effort is very sweet. Now go back to bed. Breakfast in bed is my job. You are allowed to be lazy here."

The fact that Legend didn't really feel better stuck with him, even as Legend nodded and headed back to bed. He didn't know if he was being overly sensitive or if he should be annoyed. Everything about this was new to him. He didn't have a normal to compare them to. Legend didn't date, unless it was a business arrangement. He definitely didn't date a couple. Yaro and Pytor were rich and married. Legend had twenty thousand dollars, thanks to his winnings in Vegas, and that was it. It would have been more if he hadn't refunded Henry's fee. What he had wouldn't last long. He looked around, taking in the ridiculous wealth surrounding him. Legend blew out a breath. He couldn't even make breakfast.

With his thoughts a mess, Legend crawled back into bed with Yaro. Yaro smiled and lifted the covers for him to crawl beneath.

"There is my blond Adonis. Where did you go?"

Legend did his best to keep the hurt from his voice. "I tried making breakfast, but I didn't know you are allergic to eggs."

Yaro made a sympathetic sound. "It is the thought that counts. Though it's also for the best you didn't make it all the way in here with food. Pytor is territorial over his kitchen. He is very much the hunter-gatherer."

Legend chuckled, letting his earlier aggravation go. "I see that. He didn't look thrilled."

"Pssh. Come here."

Legend scooted closer. Yaro snuggled and placed several kisses on Legend's neck and cheek until the unhappiness slipped away.

Yaro held tight. "You will see. When he gets in here with our food, he will be fine. He will look as if he has never fed us before. Cooking makes him happy. Spoiling us is his thing."

"Stay out of his kitchen. Noted."

A chuckle rumbled against his throat. "He wants to be the one who babies us. I learned long ago to just let him have it."

Sure enough, minutes later, Pytor appeared carrying a tray and puffed out like he was bringing food to bed for the first time ever. Legend found himself smiling and completely forgetting his earlier irritation. As much as it seemed like they had known each other forever, they were still learning each other's quirks. Legend could admit he was likely still sensitive from the thought of his mom hitting him earlier. Breakfast was such a small thing, and it was obviously Pytor's thing. Legend would let Pytor keep something that seemed to be important to him. There was nothing to worry about. He was reading too much into nothing.

IT WASN'T OFTEN THAT PYTOR FELT BAD, BUT HE recognized he had hurt Legend's feeling over the breakfast thing. He wasn't used to giving up control. Pytor also wasn't sure how to make it better. All Pytor knew how to do was take care of Legend so he didn't have to worry about anything anymore. They got a late start on the day, since Zander was working from home today. Lately, they had less and less to do. With Zander happily married, he didn't like going out of town often and his husband, Maverick, had Zander working from home more and more often. That left Yaro and Pytor with little to keep them busy.

Pytor left the bathroom, towel drying his hair. Legend sat on the end of the bed, lacing up his shoes. An unreasonable shot of panic hit Pytor in the chest. He still hadn't made things right from this morning. "Are you leaving?"

Legend glanced up and flashed him a smile. "I need to hit the gym."

"We have a gym here."

Legend didn't stop smiling, but neither did he back down. "I told Adrik I would pick him up from work today and we would go to the gym together to work on his self-defense lessons."

Pytor was torn right down the middle. He didn't want Legend to leave until he was one hundred percent positive they were okay, but he was leaving for Adrik. "Starting tomorrow, you will work with him here. There's no sense in taking him to the gym when we have one here and you both live here now."

"I don't live here." There was a hint of irritation in Legend's voice.

Pytor couldn't understand the problem. "You know what I mean."

Legend shook his head. "I'm not sure I do. Adrik and I go to the gym every day."

Before Pytor could find a way to express himself better, Yaro appeared in the doorway. He was dressed for the day. "There are my gorgeous men." He eyed Legend. "Are you leaving?"

Legend's chest rose and fell as if he was tired. "I'm going to pick up Adrik so we can work on his self-defense lessons."

"I will drive you."

Pytor liked this idea.

Legend shook his head. "You're dressed all nice and we're hitting the gym. Plus, I'm already running behind. Give me kisses, guys, so I can get out of here."

"Are you coming back?"

Yaro sounded sad and Pytor hated that.

Thankfully, Legend leapt to make it better. "Of course. I just need to get Adrik."

"Starting tomorrow, you will do your workout here."

Legend looked between them and shook his

head. "Did you two plan this in advance? Sheesh. Kiss me already so I can go."

Pytor decided to let things go for now. They took turns kissing Legend and setting him free. Adrik might get upset if Legend was too late. He waited until Legend was gone to broach the topic with Yaro. "I think I upset Legend."

Yaro shuffled close and wrapped his arms around Pytor's neck. His smile was everything. "He seemed fine to me. I think he was just running behind. You know that irritates me too. I like to be on time."

Even though Pytor was sure it went deeper, he had a sexy man in his arms and that always made his brain go fuzzy. "This is true. You look especially happy today. It's damn sexy."

Yaro practically bounced in place. It made Pytor's heart smile. "We have the day off. Legend won't be gone long. We could do anything. I'm also holding my sexy husband. There is a lot to smile about."

Pytor would do anything to keep Yaro's sexy smile in place. He would fix where he had gone wrong with Legend. Pytor needed his men's happiness like he needed air. Everything would be okay.

Thanks to speeding and not getting pulled over, Legend only ended up being ten minutes late. Adrik didn't seem to notice. He was all smiles as Legend came through his office door. Technically, it wasn't Adrik's office. It was Adrik's brother Justice's office. Legend secretly hoped Justice wasn't there. That dude was scary.

"Hey." Adrik came to his feet. Justice was nowhere to be seen. "I can't help but smile every time I see your face."

A smile tugged at the corners of Legend's mouth. He felt it all the way to his soul. Adrik didn't possess an ounce of artifice. Every word he said, he meant, and Legend genuinely loved him. "Are you ready to go?"

Adrik closed his laptop and moved to join Legend at the door. "Yep. Leo said he would meet us there later, so you don't have to take me home."

Legend shrugged. "I don't mind. I thought I might visit with Yaro and Pytor anyhow." Legend didn't know how to broach the topic of dating Pytor and Yaro with Adrik. First off, he wasn't one hundred percent sure of their relationship status. Secondly, it was Adrik. He was sweet, innocent, and

Legend couldn't muddy the man's waters. The knowledge that people like Adrik existed made Legend believe the world wasn't completely lost.

"You can still do that, of course." Adrik twisted his fingers as they headed for the elevator. "To be honest, I just want to see Leo." He laughed as if his confession had been ridiculous. Legend thought it was adorable. "I know we're married, and see each other all the time, I'd still rather be with him than anywhere."

Legend nodded. "I get it. My feelings aren't hurt." Plus, he really wanted to get back to Pytor and Yaro. There was a gnawing in his gut—like they had already been apart too long. If Adrik felt the same about Leo, Legend couldn't fault him for that.

The elevator stopped on the first floor and Legend caught sight of the Luna gift shop. Legend nodded toward the shop. "If you don't mind, I need to dip in this little store and grab some bottles of water. I forgot to fill my reusable bottles last night." Because he wasn't home, Legend silently added.

"Sure. There's no rush."

With Adrik at his side, Legend grabbed two bottles of water and headed for the counter. He set them by the register.

The guy working the cash register looked at the

water, glanced at him, and nodded. "Okay. Have a nice day."

Legend blinked. "I'd like to buy these."

"I'll make note of that. Have a nice day."

Legend didn't budge. This was the oddest damn thing that had ever happened to him.

Adrik sighed, grabbed the water, and passed them to Legend. He focused on the cashier as he pushed Legend toward the door. "He's still learning."

The guy chuckled while Legend let Adrik steer him from the store.

The instant they were outside, and the fresh air washed over him, Legend came back to himself. "What the fuck just happened?"

"You're part of the Kapra family," Adrik said, making air quotes around Kapra family. "You don't pay for things at any of Zander's properties. Zander takes care of it."

"But I've never even met Zander. Why would he refuse to let me pay?"

Adrik shrugged. "You were with me. Plus, you spend a lot of time with Pytor and Yaro. I'm sure people have seen you with them. Zander is the nicest person ever. So sweet, but his employees don't cross him. They won't take your money. You'll get used to it."

The bartender refusing his tip sprang to mind. Was that why Yaro and Pytor had taken him dancing at a Luna club? Were they—in essence—marking their territory? Legend didn't know how to feel. On one hand, it made him a little warm and fuzzy that his men were not only unashamed of him but wanted the world to know he was theirs. On the other hand, it seemed a bit extreme that a bartender wouldn't take his tip and he couldn't pay for water. Legend couldn't explain exactly why he was bothered. It was possible he was being overly sensitive. This was a new dynamic for him. He spent the entire drive to the gym and an hour of training with half his brain turning the topic in every direction, inspecting every angle. Adrik sneaked a couple of good hits past him in his distraction.

Leo appeared, sending Adrik scurrying. Before Legend could move, a beefy arm hooked his neck. A solid body collided with his back.

"Break my hold."

Legend's entire body melted into Pytor as Pytor's thick Russian accent caressed his ear. Everything inside him lit like a firework. "What if I don't want to?"

A sexy chuckle rumbled against his ear. "What do you want?"

"You." Legend couldn't have stopped the breathless confession if he tried in that moment.

"Damn. You do tempt me to give these unsuspecting people a show. Maybe I can lure you to the locker room instead."

Legend fought the urge to reach behind him and stroke Pytor's cock. He liked the idea of tempting him. Before he could act on his thoughts, Legend's gaze landed on Adrik. Adrik watched them, looking slightly confused. Legend did the only thing he could think to do. He held tight to Pytor's arm, dropped to one knee, and flipped Pytor to the mat. Pytor might be a big guy, but he had been unguarded, off balance, and had gravity against him. Pytor roared with laughter. Their gazes met. Legend couldn't look away or stop smiling. It was true that Pytor was overbearing, but Legend was in love with him. Pytor had more good qualities than bad. His sexy smile and laughing eyes punched Legend in the chest and went straight for his heart. Legend wanted to be with him.

"How do you always show up right when I'm missing you the most?"

Pytor's expression cleared. He crossed his arms

over his chest and made no move to get up. "Easy. I swoop in when I can't stand being away any longer, which never takes very long." He rolled and pushed to his feet. "Where are your things? I'm under strict orders from Yaro to guide you straight home." He winked. "I might have suggested it first and then Leo said he was headed this way. So I tagged along."

"It sounds like you're at my mercy." Even Legend heard the devilish intent in his voice. His gaze slid down Pytor's body, taking in the t-shirt that stretched across his chest and the jeans that protested against his large thighs. "I might do anything."

"Legend."

Legend's gaze snapped back to Pytor's face at the seriousness in his tone. He expected to get blasted by Pytor's usual heat. Instead, he caught a glimpse of Pytor's heart.

"Where are your things?"

Legend motioned toward the locker room. "In there."

With a nod, Pytor steered him in that direction. The moment they were alone and out of sight, Pytor hauled Legend inside one of the showers and yanked the curtain closed. Legend found his back against the wall and three hundred pounds of muscle in his space. Pytor kissed him—hard and deep, stealing all the oxygen from Legend. Legend held on with his heart completely engaged. Pytor changed angles and the mood shifted. There was so much sweetness in Pytor's kiss, it made Legend's teeth hurt.

"I know you were only gone two hours, but I missed this."

Legend's throat swelled at Pytor's confession. Since the first kiss, Legend had tried his damnedest not to look at things too closely or think too hard. He was scared this was temporary. It didn't feel fleeting. They felt real and damned if Legend didn't know where to go with that. It never left his mind that Yaro and Pytor were married. Legend wanted to be a part of their lives. He needed them. Whatever it took to keep them, Legend was game.

FIVE

THE DAY HAD STARTED SO AMAZING. IN FACT, THE past few weeks with Yaro and Pytor had been like a dream come true. Lately, the guys hadn't worked as much, so Legend hadn't left their sides. They had spent their days playing on the indoor warrior course, training Adrik, and simply enjoying one another. Their nights... sometimes, Legend had to stop and fan his face at the memories. Then they had gone back to work and Legend tried to go to the gym. That was where things took a turn.

"What do you mean my membership has been cancelled? I've never missed a payment here."

Johnny shook his head. "I don't know, man. That's what it says in the computer. Your membership is no longer active." He clicked some keys and tried scanning Legend's card again. "Nope. It's still saying inactive. Let me ask Chuck." He glanced around and focused on a spot over Legend's shoulder. "Hey, Chuck!"

"Yo."

"Can you come take a look at this?"

A large guy with dark hair and a thick beard came bounding over. Legend knew everyone. He had been coming there for years with no issues. Chuck tossed him a quick glance and a hey there chin bob before focusing on Johnny. "What's up?"

"Do you know anything about Legend's membership being cancelled?"

Chuck nodded. "It was cancelled online about three weeks ago." Chuck focused on Legend. "I thought maybe you'd found another gym, because those two guys you're always hanging out with—"

"Leo and Adrik?" Legend asked, interrupting him.

"Yeah. Those guys. Their memberships were cancelled too. I figured you three had decided to go elsewhere."

Three weeks ago...ugh. "I didn't cancel."

Chuck's eyebrows rose. "Weird. I mean, we can restart your membership. That's no big deal. You might want to change your password first, though. To be safe."

Legend kept nodding along with everything Chuck said while he raged internally. "Yeah." He dug out his phone. "Let me do that real quick. I also need to move some money over from savings." Maybe he would pay for an entire year so this wouldn't happen again.

Chuck patted his shoulder and went back to whatever he had been doing. Legend opened his banking app. He hadn't been home or bought anything in so long, he couldn't remember if he had enough in checking to cover that much at once. The face recognition on his phone logged him in to his account. For a moment, his brain refused to accept what his eyes showed him. Both his checking and his savings had more than six figures in each. Legend checked the account number. He was in the right account. Legend scanned his transaction history. All the money had been deposited on the same day—three weeks ago. He couldn't breathe. Pure unadulterated fury owned every cell in Legend's body. Pytor and Yaro. They just did whatever the fuck they wanted. His feelings, permission, or input had no bearing.

"I'll have to come back," Legend growled,

heading for the door. He could barely see as he ate up the ground between the building and his car. Legend texted Pytor as he went.

Legend: *Where are you right now?*

He climbed behind the wheel as he waited for a response. Legend knew he probably shouldn't drive or confront the pair in this mood, but he was about to show them a new meaning to psychotic. An odd memory sneaked in. Years ago, he had seen a woman tossing a man's things from a fifth-floor window. She laughed as his stuff crashed to the pavement below while he stood on the sidewalk begging her to stop. At the time, he had thought her completely insane. Now Legend got it. He was tempted to smash some shit. His phone buzzed.

Pytor: *At Luna. You should come by and have lunch with us. We already miss you.*

The claim sucked a bit of the wind from his sails. Legend's eyes burned. Goddamn it. Legend barely stopped himself from punching the steering wheel. He was in love with them, but there was this small pit in his stomach screaming for him to run. If they were this domineering after only a few weeks, how would they be in a few years? They were this over the top with everything going perfect. What would they do if things went bad? Should he be scared?

They had to talk. He needed them to hear him. Legend felt like... he couldn't describe how he felt. All he knew was, they weren't equal.

Legend: *I'm on my way*.

Pytor: *We'll meet you at the restaurant on the third floor*.

With a deep breath for courage, Legend headed that way. Through the fifteen-minute drive, he concentrated on breathing. Legend didn't know where to begin. When he tried saying the words aloud, he sounded ridiculous. "Hey, you know how I'm not allowed to make breakfast or pay for anything, which is stupid since you dumped more than half a mil in my bank account? Yeah, I don't like that."

Legend growled. He wasn't crazy. People didn't hack into other people's accounts, cancel their memberships, and put money in their bank. Fuck. Legend rubbed his forehead. People had been buying him for years. He didn't want that with Pytor and Yaro. Legend knew everything they did came from a good place. Possibly.

As the valet came into view, Legend realized he was dressed for the gym and not a fancy restaurant with a dress code. Another loud snort escaped him. Well, he was about to test how much the staff would overlook for a Kapra family member. He got his ticket and headed for the door. Legend held the frayed edges of his anger all the way to the restaurant.

A man in a black and white suit headed his way. "Mr. Perry. Your table is this way." If the guy noticed Legend's bright red sports tights and tank top, he didn't bat an eyelash.

Legend spotted Pytor and Yaro at a table in the corner. His resolve slipped. They were so beautiful. Two sets of eyes watched his approach with happiness lighting them from the inside out. Legend didn't know how to fight when even he didn't understand why he was so bothered.

They came to their feet as he reached the table and took turns brushing their lips across his. As Legend sat across from them at the small round table, their feet found his beneath and a smile tugged at Legend's lips. Goddamn them.

"All heads turned your way as you crossed the room," Yaro said, sounding proud.

"That's because I'm out of dress code."

Pytor snorted. "It is because you are beautiful. What have you done with your morning?"

At the question, Legend took a breath. It was now or never.

"Is that Henry Krill?" Yaro asked, staring at some point behind Legend.

Legend fought the urge to look. Yaro's expression had already hardened. Legend didn't want to make things worse.

Pytor's face darkened. "Yes. It is. He looks as if he can't decide if he should approach or not."

Yaro was practically snarling. "I would truly hate to break his legs today and ruin lunch."

"What did Henry do to you?" Even though Henry was the last person Legend ever wanted to see again, he didn't think the man had ever done anything to Pytor or Yaro.

They ignored him. "He sees all three of us as employees and wants to storm over here to demand time with Legend, but he's also terrified, as he should be." They were talking about Legend as if he wasn't there.

Pytor nodded. "I should go tell him that Legend is no longer for hire."

"Says who?" Legend said, feeling his temper slip. All of his earlier anger came rushing back. "I never agreed to quit my job."

Pytor finally focused on him. "Yaro and I decided you won't be doing that anymore. You belong to us and you no longer need the money."

He didn't even try to hide that he had dumped that money in Legend's account.

"Also, you will move in with us. There is no reason for you to keep a separate house," Yaro said, adding his thoughts. He looked Pytor's way. "We should talk to Zander when we get back upstairs."

Pytor nodded, looking thoughtful. "Agreed, even though he won't likely notice a new addition to the house."

Neither man acknowledged Legend at all as they planned his life. As usual, it was like he wasn't there for the decision-making. It hit Legend. He was their pet. They didn't need his thoughts or desires, only his acquiescence. He was expected to do as they ordered. The pit that had been growing in his gut widened.

"Oh, we should get him a new phone so he's not inundated with calls and texts from upset ex clients."

Yaro nodded at Pytor's suggestion. "You're right. He does not need to listen to their whining and begging."

Legend slammed his hand on the table, making the silverware rattle and bringing all eyes their way. "Enough." He squeezed the spot between his eyes where a pain bloomed. Legend took a breath and tried to be calm. At least they were looking at him.

He ran his tongue over his teeth and dove in, picking a place to start with no idea where this was headed. All Legend knew was, he was miserable, and he needed this to stop. "Do you two even hear yourselves?" Legend took a breath and started over. "You know I used to think I would make someone an amazing husband. I always wanted to be a dad too, but that's another story." A smile touched Legend's lips, and—for a moment—he wondered if his mind had finally snapped from all the bullshit he had dealt with in the past few years. "Then I met you two," Legend's smile slipped away, "and I tossed every dream I ever had for myself aside. I started flirting and preening, hoping for I don't even know what. I gave up everything I had and everything I wanted to take a chance on you." Legend fought for air. This was so much harder than he ever dreamed. He loved them, but they didn't love him. Not really. "The thing is," Legend said, feeling the sting of tears prick at his eyes. "I didn't mind that I had to give up a few minor things—like making you two breakfast or buying you roses. Yeah, I tried to do that the other day, while explaining they were a gift, and the guy threatened to call one of you to be sure it was okay for me to spend my money. But still, I was okay, because I thought I was gaining so much more. But I wasn't gaining anything. I've just been disappearing a little more every day to make you both more." He pushed to his feet. "Next time you want to give some love away, adopt a dog. You don't want what you have with me. You don't want a free-thinking person." He walked away, leaving his men behind. His heart broke a little more with every step. He could feel the two coming after him—like a physical thing. Legend didn't slow. He needed to get his car from valet and get lost.

"Legend. Hold up."

"Talk to us," Yaro added.

Legend picked up speed. A growl rose in Legend's throat as Henry unexpectedly stepped into his path. Legend lifted his eyes to the heavens, because really, this could not be happening.

"I've been trying to get ahold of you, but you're not answering my calls or texts, and your website is down."

Legend barely stopped himself from glancing Pytor and Yaro's way, but he could feel their stares boring into his skin. If they ever talked to him about any damn thing, they would know he had already stopped working. "Okay." He was too angry to gather his thoughts for a brighter response.

"If you have a minute, I'd like to explain what happened in Vegas."

No. This definitely couldn't be happening. Legend knew Henry wouldn't think twice about speaking his mind in front of Yaro and Pytor. They were like the maid or whatever to him. They weren't real—beneath his notice, but Legend knew they were there. He knew they were hanging on every word.

"There's nothing to explain. You made me an offer, finding an underhanded way to get what you wanted from me, and now you're done. If you think you're the first to play games and use me, think again. In fact, there's a line forming today. Now, if you'll excuse me, I was already in the middle of storming away from one argument."

Henry wasn't having it. He stepped sideways, continuing to block Legend's path when Legend tried walking around him. "That's not what happened at all. My marriage proposal was genuine. I just over thought things, the way I always do. That's why I came to your room that night. I wanted to be sure I could really deal with living the rest of my life with someone who only wants my money. Then, you sideswiped me by sweeping me into bed. I never expected you might really want me for me. That messed with me more than I like to admit."

"Marriage proposal?" Pytor growled.

Yaro jumped on the second part. "Swept him into bed?"

Legend snapped. He turned on the pair with every bit of rage that had been building inside him all day. "You two have no room to balk about any damn thing. Not only are you already married, I'm sure you had no qualms about leaving me that night to spend the night fucking each other, because—as I previously pointed out—you're already married to each other. You already have everything I never will," Legend said, stabbing himself in the chest with his thumb. A breathless note entered his hostile tone as Legend recognized what hurt him most. Losing him wouldn't matter to them. They would always have each other. "For fuck's sake. This doesn't have anything to do with you. And why can't you two be on my side for once? Is it not enough that I'll always be just the third wheel? Fuck it. It's always going to be you two against me. Ugh." He made a sweeping gesture, on the verge of unspeakable rage. "I've obviously made a lot of mistakes between the three of you. You have no idea how sick I am of being wrong about people. I'm tired of only being everyone's fucking pet. Did any one of you stop to think maybe I have dreams too? I have things I want. Did any of you consider that I might want the one fucking thing I don't have?" Legend walked away, leaving everyone behind, and muttering to himself, because he was too upset to stop. "I've never been so goddamn tired in my whole goddamn life. Somehow, I have got to get the fuck out of this soul-sucking town. Leave all these selfish motherfuckers in the dust." He was half a second away from kicking things over in his path. All Legend wanted was a home and a family that belonged to him, and all he ever found was bullshit. It was exhausting. He couldn't do this for one more day.

YARO HADN'T SAID A WORD SINCE LEGEND walked away. It was terrifying. There had been very few times he had seen Yaro this upset, and they had been through some horrible shit no one should have to see. They could have gone after Legend. Pytor thought they should have, but Yaro had stood like a statue, watching Legend walk away before stonily swinging his gaze between Pytor and Henry. Then he had walked away. Yaro reclaimed their table, paid their bill, and then went back to work. Pytor knew his husband well and his hard mask hid a storm of emotions that could spill at any moment in any form.

The moment they were alone inside their bedroom, Pytor broke. He couldn't take the silence any longer. Pytor couldn't take the guilt. "We should go find him."

Yaro yanked open the dresser drawer with enough force Pytor expected it to fall apart in his hand. He kept his face turned away as he pulled out some clothes. "You don't want to know what I think."

"Yes, I do. We have to be together on this—like all things."

Yaro tossed him a glance that should have killed him on the spot. "Did you not hear anything he said? Being together on everything drove him away. We are so fucking together on everything, he felt unwelcome. This is not what he needs. We are not what he wants. The right thing to do is to let Henry give him the life he deserves."

It was like being stabbed repeatedly. "What he deserves is us. Henry does not love him. We do."

With one last annoyed look his way, Yaro disappeared inside the bathroom, closing and locking the door behind him. Pytor stood and stared at the wooden object between them. They had never closed the bathroom door. In truth, Pytor hadn't realized their bathroom even had a door. He was learning all sorts of new and horrible things today.

YARO STOOD BENEATH THE STEADY STREAM OF water falling from the rain ceiling. He stared at nothing, seeing nothing but Legend's face. Yaro saw it now, as he sifted through every memory. He saw Legend's expression every time they had made him the outsider. Each time they had made a decision without consulting him. Every time he had tried to please them, only to have them take away his chance. Yaro wrapped his arms around his middle. They didn't deserve Legend. He had tried so hard. They had done nothing but shove their decisions down his throat.

Yaro's eyes fell closed. The urge to hunt him down and beg for mercy and forgiveness was crippling. That was just another selfish desire. Legend deserved to be set free from their greedy grip. Yaro didn't know how to fix them any other way. Pytor and Yaro were already married, as Legend kept pointing out. They couldn't marry him. Yaro was too old to be talking about having kids. Plus, Legend was right. Yaro hadn't thought to ask if

Legend wanted those things. He felt like the lowest piece of shit on the planet, because he was, and he had been more than ready to deny Legend everything Yaro already had for himself. Why? That was the question that ate at Yaro's soul. Why hadn't he considered Legend at all? Maybe he had known, deep down, that Legend would say exactly what he had today. He wanted a husband and kids. A young man's life. They had nothing to offer him. That meant he had stayed as long as he had because he had chosen them over his dreams. Yaro's chin dropped. His gaze hit the shower floor. His eyes burned. He had tried so hard—despite everything that tried breaking him over the years—to be a good man. Yaro didn't feel like a good man now. Pytor yanked open the shower door, bringing Yaro's head up.

"How can you lock a door against me?"

Yaro went back to staring at the floor. "I want to be alone."

"You're the only friend I have, and I don't want to be alone."

A lump formed in Yaro's throat, making him wonder if tears mixed with the water running down his face. "Maybe neither of us deserves to get what we want."

He had wanted so badly to take away the unhappiness he had seen in Legend's eyes when they met. That was it. Yaro never meant to make him worse. Yet he had seen the growing misery in Legend since they took over his life. They didn't deserve happiness.

"We have to fix this."

That was Pytor in a nutshell. He was a doer. "I think we've done enough fixing." Even Yaro heard the way it sounded, like he had been chewing on glass.

"Do you think I'm a bad person? Are you finally done with me?"

Yaro's head spun from lack of oxygen. That was how hard Pytor's question hit him. In all their years together, Pytor had never—not once—insinuated they might be over. Yaro fell apart. He couldn't breathe. He was not the type of person who hurt people. In fact, Yaro had taken many lashes with a bullwhip over the years for protecting Zander and Hendrix from the Conti. It wasn't in his nature to damage an innocent soul. Yet he had made Legend's life worse.

Pytor stepped beneath the water with him—clothes and all—to hold him. His arms squeezed Yaro tight, even as his fingers trailed lightly up and down

Yaro's spine. "We will talk to him, and we will make everything better. You will see. You will be proud to be my husband again. I won't fail you."

Yaro shook harder. "I'm not disappointed in you. I'm ashamed of me. We did everything he accused us of doing. I would never hurt you the way I hurt him. Why did I do it? If you teamed up with him to shut me out, I would die. Why would I do that to someone else I love? I am a bad person."

Pytor shushed him. "Stop saying that. You are not bad. We are still learning. He needs to learn to talk to us openly, and we need to learn to let go of our control. But we will fucking learn together. We love him. He cannot leave without hearing our apology."

Yaro's chest eased a little more with every word Pytor said. He nodded against the man's shoulder. They would make this right. Yaro couldn't live with any other outcome. The three of them were a set. Since the day they met Legend, Legend had been slowly tying his life to theirs. Without Legend, Yaro wasn't sure they would feel whole again.

SIX

The constant feeling of defeat that Yaro carried around since Legend walked away doubled as he stared at the *for sale* sign in Legend's yard. There was already a *sold* sign slapped over it and the place was empty. That much they knew only because Pytor was excellent at breaking and entering. Legend was gone.

It was possible he had moved right down the road or was staying with a friend. Hell, maybe Henry had beat them to the apology punch and already convinced Legend to marry him. It was entirely possible Legend sold his house weeks ago, and they wouldn't know because they never listened. They had no way of knowing the answers because Legend wasn't answering their calls or texts. Most likely, he had blocked their numbers. Loss washed over Yaro anew. Pytor squeezed his hand. Yaro swallowed down the grief.

"We will ask for help," Pytor said, surprising Yaro. Pytor never asked for help. "Leo or Whiskey will know where to start."

Yaro nodded. This was a good plan. Both Leo and Whiskey had worked as detectives for years. Surely they would know what to do. If not, Yaro didn't know what move to make.

"I should have chased after him at Luna." Yaro's throat tightened around the confession.

"No. You were right to stop us. He was too angry. I'm not sure there was anything we could say then to fix things. He needed time."

Yaro took a breath. They would not stop until they found Legend and made everything okay. "We will find him." Even Yaro heard the determination in his voice. Legend had stolen their hearts. They would not let him disappear now. Love meant fighting for one another. It meant staying and making things work. They would make this work. Yaro couldn't accept anything else.

It was absolute hell waiting for his opening. Pytor stared at Zander, mentally willing the man to get to the end of his phone call so they could talk. Even though he could clearly remember Zander as a child, he looked imposing sitting behind his desk now. He had grown into an amazing man. Pytor and Yaro had been his private security since he was sixteen. They had only been eighteen at the time, but they had felt much older thanks to the Conti's abuse. This was the first time they had needed or asked for Zander's help. Zander disconnected his call and leaned closer to the paperwork spread across his desk. Leo and Adrik huddled on the couch in the corner, working on Adrik's studies. They kept stealing kisses when they thought no one watched.

"I need to ask a favor."

Everyone in the room froze despite Pytor's attempt at speaking quietly. It was obvious everyone recognized he never asked for anything.

Zander blinked for a moment before visibly fighting off the shock. "Anything you need, of course."

"May we use Leo or Whiskey to find Legend?"

"Who in the hell is Legend?"

It was Pytor's turn to blink at Zander in confusion. "He's been to the house a million times."

"Why didn't you ask me?" Adrik asked before Zander had time to respond.

Pytor honestly hadn't considered Adrik, but that was a fair point. Adrik had his attention, but Yaro beat him to the punch. "Do you know where he's gone? He's not answering our texts and his house has sold."

Adrik looked every bit as surprised by the news as they had been. "Really?"

"Seriously. Who the hell is Legend?" Zander asked, still sounding confused.

"He is ours," Yaro answered absently.

A line appeared between Adrik's brows. "What do you mean?"

"When did this happen?" Zander said at the same time.

Leo visibly tried suppressing a smile as he rubbed Adrik's leg. "I'll explain later, baby. You text Legend and see what you can find out. Just don't mention Pytor or Yaro. Okay?"

Adrik nodded and started typing on his phone.

Zander didn't let things go as easily as Adrik. "Explain." The bite in his voice let Pytor know he wasn't playing.

Pytor glanced Yaro's way. Yaro flashed him a

supportive smile. Pytor took a breath, focused on Zander, and started the only place he could. "Adrik brought Legend to the house once, and we liked him a lot, so we invited him to run through the warrior course with us. He fit in. Just like one of us, and so we kept inviting him back. He kept showing up. Then, one day, we were doing the stretches, warming up to play. Legend poked us in the chests and said, 'I swear you're both even bigger today.' Yaro became the jokester and said, 'You're smaller.'" Pytor shook his head, trying to explain the unexplainable. They had felt something that day. "All the beauty and light drained from him—like a mask fell. He said, 'I think I get a little smaller every single day.' Yaro and I looked at each other. It was like we shared thoughts." Yaro reached over and grabbed Pytor's hand, slipping his fingers through Pytor's, lending his strength. Pytor said what they hadn't truly voiced aloud about that day. "We have always had more love than most couples. Enough to share and not be less. Legend needs us and we won't watch him drown. But you know us. We are too much, and he disappeared."

"Oooh," Adrik said, dragging out the word and obviously catching on. He was so sweet and innocent. "He moved to Texas."

Pytor's head whipped around at the announcement. "What?" Even he heard the bite in his bark. Pytor was incapable of toning it down.

Thankfully, Adrik didn't look upset. He nodded. "He texted me that he's in Texas, which reminded me that he'd already told me he was thinking about moving there a few months back. He has some friends there that are starting an escort service, Cubs for Rent. I thought that was cute and Legend laughed at me, which is pretty common when he talks about work."

Pytor tried to keep up, even though his temper was through the roof and his heart was in his throat. "He moved to Texas to work for an escort service."

Adrik shook his head. "No. He said he was tired of being nothing but arm candy, but he has an extensive client list and he's not good at anything or smart enough to do anything else. So he planned to help other people get off the ground, doing what he did. I thought he planned to go about three months ago, but then he didn't. So I thought he'd changed his mind and then I didn't think about it again."

Yaro squeezed Pytor's hand. Pytor knew he felt the same panic. He knew in his heart Legend had gone to Texas to get away from them. He was gone. While Texas was only a plane ride away, it was the significance of the move that Pytor couldn't shake. Legend wasn't waiting for them. He didn't expect them to be okay. Legend didn't consider this split temporary. He was done with them. Pytor couldn't breathe. He had done this to them. As much as he wanted Legend, he hadn't let Legend in. He had refused to let go of even an ounce of control. In his heart, Pytor knew everything he did had been to make Legend's life easier, but he should have used his words.

"Find out an address, please? I have to go fix this."

"Hold up," Zander said, pulling the plug. "You're not going anywhere until we talk about this."

Pytor growled in his frustration. He loved Zander and owed him a lot, but Zander would not stop them from this.

Zander held up a hand, stopping Pytor before his temper snapped. "Just hear me out, okay. If you're serious about this guy, then you need to take a breath. He ran for a reason. You say you were too much. What did you two do?"

Pytor and Yaro exchanged a pained look. Yaro answered. "A lot. We took over his life without his say so."

Zander covered his eyes. "Okay," he said, taking

a breath before dropping his hands and focusing on them again. "Let me guess. You did exactly what I did with Maverick and tried to make his life better by helping him behind the scenes and without his permission?"

They nodded.

Zander rolled his eyes. "You both had already seen how that worked out for me."

Pytor rushed to defend them. "It wasn't exactly the same. We did not try to convince him everything was his idea."

"That's right," Yaro said, backing him up. "We just told him how things would be."

Zander stared at them expressionlessly.

Leo snorted.

Thankfully, Adrik came to the rescue. "I didn't have to ask for an address. He says Cubs for Rent is having an opening night ball and he wants me to come and then stay the weekend." He glanced Leo's way. "Is that okay?"

Leo transformed into the person who always saved Adrik. "I'm fine with you visiting Legend, but is it okay with you? That's a long way from here and you'd be surrounded by a lot of strange men."

"Yaro and Pytor will go with Adrik," Zander

announced. "They will keep him safe and use the event as a way to get back their man." Pytor stared at Zander with hope in his heart. Zander looked so confident of every word he spoke. "But you will not force him back here," Zander said, his voice turning hard. "Hear me and learn from my mistakes. If you two love this man, sit down and be honest. Explain why life has made you unbending. If he loves you, he will understand and find a way to make it work. But you will not race to Texas and make things worse. It would break my heart to see him crush you. I love you both too much."

Pytor knew Zander was right. They needed to use their heads this time around. He focused on Adrik. "Are you okay with us tagging along?"

For a moment, Adrik chewed his bottom lip, looking worried. Pytor wasn't sure the problem had anything to do with them.

Leo rubbed Adrik's thigh. "How about this? I'll go with you to Texas and stay at a nearby hotel. When the party is over, if you don't feel like staying or get scared, I'll come get you."

Adrik visibly relaxed. "Okay. If you're okay with doing all that, I would feel better with you there."

Hope rose in Pytor's chest. Yaro squeezed his

hand. They were on the same page. Legend was almost within their grasp again. Pytor just hoped he had the patience to wait, because he couldn't fuck this up.

SEVEN

LEGEND SWITCHED HIS ATTENTION BETWEEN watching the clock for Adrik's arrival and finishing up the final details for tonight's ball. He was a nervous wreck. Legend couldn't recall the last time he had slept more than a few hours at a time. Actually, he could, but Legend couldn't let himself think about Pytor and Yaro. He was always a single breath away from a complete breakdown. Legend couldn't let that happen. He had lost too much in the past year. If Legend ever let that wall down, grief would swallow him.

Toby crossed the room, looking completely calm for someone who would be on display tonight—like being circled by hawks. Of course, Toby—like his brothers—had every reason to be confident. They were big, sexy, and didn't really need anyone else. The triplets were identical to almost the tiniest of details. They looked like men who could fix a car while listening to someone's feelings and then fuck those feelings away. They would be great at this. When this night was over, Legend had no clue how he would distract himself next.

"Tanner and Tucker are finished with the guest rooms. Shouldn't your friend be here by now?"

Legend glanced at his watch. "Any minute."

Toby snagged Legend's waist and walked Legend closer until they were hip to hip. His forest green eyes filled with concern. "Are you okay? You look ready to drop."

"I'm good. Promise. I just want your night to be perfect. If this goes as planned, you'll have a full client list and word of mouth, spreading your praises."

A wicked smile touched Toby's lips. "You know, things could have been so much different for us. If you had fallen madly in love with me—the way I wanted—we could be cozied up in a cabin somewhere, drinking wine and making love by the fire."

Legend wrapped his arms around Toby's neck

and held on. He couldn't help but smile at Toby's description. "I'd get bored in two days."

A gasp of mock outrage escaped Toby. His hands found Legend's ass. Somehow, he managed to haul Legend even closer. "I resent that. You have no idea how creative I can be." He scorched Legend with a hot look. "You'd lose your voice after two days."

Toby spread happiness everywhere he went. Legend couldn't stop smiling. "Okay. I amend my statement. You'd get bored after two days."

In an instant, Toby transformed from playful to serious. "I accept your challenge." Legend's mind went blank. Toby meant every word. Just as fast as it happened, Toby's serious tone fell away. He released a loud and dramatic sigh. "I know you already love someone else. It's a stiff blow." He winked. "But I can take all the stiff things life throws my way."

Legend stroked Toby's dark hair before pulling away. "Tart."

Toby hissed like a cat. "Hussy."

The doorbell rang and a stampede of booted feet running for the door filled the house. Everyone wanted to be the first to greet Adrik. Legend shook his head and headed for the foyer. Poor Adrik. He had no clue what he was stepping into. Legend cleared the archway of the foyer in time to see the door swing wide. Adrik stood on the other side with his suitcase. He wore baggy jeans and old band t-shirt. His hair was a mess and he rubbed his arm, looking nervous. He was the most beautiful sight for sore eyes.

Legend pushed his way past the triplets, snatched up Adrik, and rocked him side to side, acting ridiculous in a way that he reserved solely for the awkward adorable man who made Legend smile like no one else did, because he didn't see Legend in a sexual light in any way, shape, or form.

"Adrik!" He kissed the man's cheek just to watch him blush and swipe at his cheek. "I'm so happy to see a familiar face."

"What are we?" Pytor asked with a sly smile, appearing behind him, dragging another suitcase.

"Do we not count?" Yaro added, closely on Pytor's heels. The way they smiled... fuck. Legend had never been so sideswiped by anyone and they fucking knew it.

Adrik motioned their way. "I hope it's okay they tagged along. Leo wouldn't let me come alone. Also, I figured the more sexy men you had at this thing, the better."

"It's fine." Legend kept his smile in place. Not only was he incapable of showing any weakness, he couldn't let someone as innocent as Adrik be exposed to what he had done. He never wanted Adrik to know he had stepped in the middle of someone's marriage. "There are plenty of rooms here. I'm sure the guys will be thrilled to have the extra bodies." He glanced behind him at the triplets. They waited patiently for introductions. "Right, guys?"

The triplets eyed Pytor and Yaro with open curiosity. "We'll make room."

Legend stepped aside and motioned Adrik inside. He tried not to breathe in Yaro and Pytor's scent as they passed. Instead, he stayed focused on Adrik. Adrik was who he had invited. If Pytor and Yaro wanted to come along to keep Adrik safe, Legend couldn't stop them. He had never been able to stop them from doing anything they wanted.

As everyone crowded inside the front room, Legend motioned toward the triplets. "Adrik, meet Toby, Tucker, and Tanner Kodiak. They're the guys I'm helping to start their business."

Adrik shook their hands. "Oh, wow. Please tell me there's a way to tell you apart. I'm already really bad with names and painfully awkward. It's likely I'll call you anything."

Legend completely understood. He had known the three forever. That was the only way he could tell the triplets apart. They had vastly different personalities that shone brightly in their looks.

Tucker laughed. "Sure. I'm the best-looking."

Tanner nodded. "I have the sexiest voice."

Toby winked. "I'm the best in bed, but since you're married..."

A nervous-sounding chuckle escaped Adrik. "Um. Okay."

All three men automatically looked contrite at Adrik's open discomfort. They were good at reading people. Unfortunately, they hadn't been quick enough at reading Adrik and Legend hadn't thought to warn them. Tanner was the first to try to fix things. He held up his wrist. "It's not much help, but I have a tattoo on my wrist."

Toby pointed at his face. "I have a scar under my eye from an old hockey injury."

Adrik visibly relaxed. His smile turned less pained. "I'll do my best."

"Who are your friends?" Toby asked, eyeing Yaro and Pytor.

Adrik motioned behind him. "These are my friends, Pytor and Yaro." All three triplets' heads turned his way before looking away every bit as quickly. Legend fought a blush. It couldn't have been more obvious he had told the guys everything. Adrik kept talking, oblivious. "I really hope it's okay for them to be here. They're very pretty and I hoped they might look the part of potential customers tonight. Kind of like when everyone's crowding around a display at the store and everyone else does too just to see what everyone else is looking at, if that makes sense."

Tucker nodded. "That's a great idea." He eyed the men like meat. "They would make us look desired and sought after."

"Exactly," Adrik said, sounding bright.

"In that case," Tanner said, coming to Legend's rescue. "We'll steal them away, find them a room, and practice our pitch."

They tried urging Yaro and Pytor toward the stairs. The pair didn't budge. Instead, they held their ground while staring a hole in Legend's head, openly waiting to be acknowledged. Legend gave in and looked their way.

Yaro moved closer and took Legend's hand. He brought it to his lips. "Until tonight, sexy."

Pytor waited his turn. After Yaro made a show of stroking Legend's wrist, Pytor took his hand. His tongue shot out, lightly stroking Legend's wrist. Legend couldn't look away. He was glad for his untucked flannel, because he went hard immediately at the heat in Pytor's eyes. Legend already knew what that tongue could do. It wasn't fair for them to be so much of everything when they didn't really want him to be a part of them.

Pytor's lips brushed the same spot his tongue had. "We'll find you later." Funny how it sounded like a threat. Finally, they let the triplets lead them away.

Legend's gaze slid Adrik's way. He was openly staring.

"They touch everyone." Legend felt himself blush. Adrik was too innocent to witness this.

Adrik shrugged. "Really, they don't. They touch each other and you, but that's it."

"They're just being nice." Legend didn't know why he couldn't let it go. It just seemed wrong for Adrik to know he had touched them.

For a moment, Adrik stared at him in silence. He didn't smirk or judge. Instead, Adrik's quiet acceptance was freeing. "No, they're not. They want you. No one knows better than you that I'm the most clueless person on the planet, and even I know they want you. Even if I couldn't see it, they told me so."

A deep sadness touched Legend's soul. Despite always being treated like a whore, he had always believed he was a good person, until Yaro and Pytor.

104

Adrik was the only person Legend could talk to about this. "They're married."

Adrik's expression let Legend know he took this seriously. "I guess that makes you really special, then. If I think about anyone else touching Leo, I want to commit murder. Surely it's the same for Yaro and Pytor. Yet they chose you and are willing to risk a long and happy marriage. You must be worth it to them."

Legend couldn't believe he was talking to Adrik, of all people, about this. There was no one else, so he admitted something he never had. "Doing what I do, I'm not ashamed. Countless times I've been treated like a whore by people because of my job, even though I don't have sex for money, but I have never been ashamed of myself. Until Pytor and Yaro."

Adrik's clear expression never changed. He was unabashedly willing to discuss this with no discomfort clouding his features. It was nice. Freeing. Adrik's hands lifted and fell, as if to show he had nothing. "If you're embarrassed, you're the only one. Pytor and Yaro sat in a room filled with their closest friends and declared you are theirs. It was one of the bravest things I've ever seen. They're not afraid for anyone to know about you." Adrik looked so sure of every word, Legend couldn't stop hanging on every one of them. "If you have feelings for them too, I think you should take a chance. Yaro and Pytor are two of the best people I know. They're full of life and love. It's beautiful." Adrik looked a bit sad as he said the words—like he didn't see himself in the same light as he willingly described others. That thought hurt Legend's heart. Adrik was one of the best people he knew. Possibly, he was the best. Life had tried ripping everything from him, including his humanity. Instead of folding, Adrik rose from the ashes like a phoenix.

He brushed away talk of men he would likely never have again. "You're beautiful. Look at you," he said, turning outrageous once again. He took Adrik's hands and held them as he openly inspected Adrik's body, despite the man's blushing. "You've always been ten times hotter than everyone else, but I can tell you've been working on the ninja course with the guys. I bet you're kicking everyone's ass."

"Stop." Adrik sounded horrified and embarrassed. "I look exactly the same." He truly was adorable in his awkwardness. Legend thought Adrik was the most endearing person on the planet. He envied Adrik's husband, Leo.

A wave of sadness washed over Legend. "Maybe you do. It's really hard to improve on perfection.

Since Leo isn't here, would you like to be my date tonight? That way, neither of us has to be alone."

Adrik smiled sweetly. "If you're alone, then yes. But if you're not, my feelings won't be hurt. I know your men come first."

Legend tried to smile. They weren't his men. Not anymore. "Let me show you to your room. I put you next door to me. That way, if you decide in the middle of the night that you made a terrible mistake by marrying Leo, I'm only a few steps away."

Adrik rolled his eyes, but he let Legend lead him away. "You're ridiculous."

Only with Adrik. Plus, it was a mask. Legend felt like a million-year-old mummy on the inside—dust held together by string. Despite all that, he really cared about Adrik and Leo had warned him Adrik might not do well sleeping away from the familiar. Concentrating on keeping Adrik's sanity safe also kept Legend from going insane. Yaro and Pytor were here. Under the same roof. Legend might not make it through the night.

He snagged Adrik's bag and headed for the stairs. "Come on. I'll show to your room. Actually, it's adjoining to mine. I'll keep my side unlocked, just in case," he said with a wink.

Adrik blushed again, but he fell in step with Legend.

Adrik didn't say anything else until they were alone inside his room. Adrik looked around before focusing on Legend. "This is nice. Can I ask you a dumb question?"

Legend didn't hesitate. "You're never dumb, but of course."

"What's your real name?"

Okay. That was a weird question. "Um... Legend."

The smile that snapped to Adrik's face was irresistible. "Oh, ha. I've always thought that's just what people called you because you're so good at everything."

Legend found himself blinking back an unexpected wave of tears. Adrik had no clue how much Legend needed someone like Adrik in his life. He liked to pretend he was over the top conceited. In truth, Legend sucked at everything. The only thing he had ever felt confident doing was making other people feel good about themselves. Unfortunately, he didn't feel good about himself. "You're incredibly kind. I hope you know that."

Adrik sat on the end of his bed, giving Legend his full attention. "You are too. I'm not surprised

Yaro and Pytor fell for you. They haven't had many people be nice to them over the years. I imagine you're irresistible to them. Is it okay if I ask you something else?"

Legend crossed the room and flopped down on Adrik's bed, stomach first. Adrik turned and sat crossed legged beside him. Legend propped up his head with his hand and settled in. He wanted to spend time with Adrik. "Shoot."

Adrik plucked at the comforter. He didn't meet Legend's stare. "Why didn't you tell me that you were dating Yaro and Pytor? I thought we were friends. But you had a lot going on, and then you moved away, but you didn't say a word to me about any of it."

It hurt Legend's chest that Adrik sounded genuinely injured by Legend's silence. Legend shrugged, feeling exposed. It was his turn to pluck at the comforter. "I don't know. For a long time, I didn't really have any friends. I couldn't let myself be real or get close to anyone who paid me for dates, and I worked every weekend. That made it hard to make friends. Then, my mom got sick. My time was split between working and helping her. I guess I got used to not talking to anyone about anything that mattered." Legend swallowed. His throat hurt.

"Then she died." Legend swallowed again. This was a lot harder than he would have expected. "I don't know. No one was there for me, and I guess I don't really know how to stop being alone."

"Okay." Adrik sounded so accepting. It was getting harder for Legend not to cry. "I didn't have a childhood. So I don't know how to be friends and I thought—maybe—I was doing it wrong."

A sad smile tugged at the corners of Legend's mouth. "No. You're doing great." Legend sat up and matched Adrik's cross-legged pose. With his elbows on his knees, Legend tried to put his thoughts into words. "At first, before anything happened between us, I was ashamed of the way I felt about Pytor and Yaro. I knew they were married, and I had no intention of getting in the middle of that, but neither could I stay away. Then, as soon as our feelings were out there, I knew almost immediately that something wasn't right between us. I didn't want to admit it and I couldn't put my finger on what was wrong, but I knew in my heart our relationship wouldn't last." Legend shrugged. "I guess I thought, since it couldn't last, I would keep what we were as a secret memory just for me." Legend swallowed. He still hadn't stopped hurting, and he didn't think he ever would.

"You love them." Adrik sounded sure and not the least bit judgmental.

Legend smiled. "I have for a long time, but I'm not sure that's enough."

"You should talk it out. I know it sounds like such a simple fix, but it works. When I talk, and Leo hears me, that's when I know we'll always be fine."

Legend bit back a huff. "They don't hear me, though. That's the problem. Do you know, they hacked my bank account and put eight hundred and forty thousand dollars in my account without saying a word to me? I don't even know how to go about giving back that much money."

Adrik didn't bat an eye at the number. He nodded, looking every bit as serious and involved as he had from the moment they sat down. "If you knew what they've had to do over the years to get that money, you would realize how much that shows their love for you. I'm not taking sides. I'm just saying, they are from a world you can't even begin to imagine, but they should have tried to explain that to you instead of simply dumping a ton of money on you. Trust me, I know it's frustrating. I asked Zander if I could work full time to make more money. He said no and then put two million in my account without asking. The difference is, I know the price they paid to have that much money to freely give. I know, because I paid the same price with no gain." Adrik held his stare, looking so serious that Legend couldn't look away. "When you come from a really dark and screwed-up place, and you meet someone like you—happy, light... good." Adrik shook his head. "You just want to give everything to make sure they never see what you have. You want them to stay happy and carefree—like keeping a child innocent. But the three of you need to have a real conversation, because you love each other enough to share your lives, and that means sharing everything. Even the ugly stuff." Adrik straightened his spine. A smile stretched his lips. "So don't be afraid to throw something heavy at their thick heads to get their attention. They can take it."

Legend couldn't help but smile at the image Adrik's words painted. "We'll see. Until then, though, be my date tonight. There'll be a room filled with my ex-clients and I'm done entertaining people. I just want to spend time with my friend."

Adrik flashed a shy smile. "Okay. I'll keep you safe."

Legend bit the inside of his cheek to keep from laughing. Adrik was an awesome human. Legend wouldn't forget it again. Even if he never returned to

California, Legend would find a way to still spend time with Adrik. They were friends for life.

———

THE THREE IDENTICAL MEN WHO HAD SHOWN them to their room now blocked the door. Their arms were crossed over their chests and they wore matching scowls. It was adorable. Yaro fought the urge to pat their heads. Pytor could snap their legs without breaking a sweat, but it was cute they thought to defend Legend.

"Are we to get the lecture now?" Yaro asked as he wheeled his suitcase to the corner of the room. Since the house was just that—a house. It was a nice house that anyone would love to own. But their room wasn't big enough for all the huge bodies crowding the space and their luggage.

"No lecture."

Yaro had no idea which man it was. They all looked alike. "Which one are you again?"

"Toby," he answered absently, motioning for the other two to leave. "I'll be fine. Keep an eye out for Legend." With a final narrow-eyed glance their way, the other two brothers stepped out, leaving them alone with their obvious leader.

Yaro moved to a chair by the window and sat, while Pytor continued standing guard. If Yaro knew nothing else, he knew his husband. Pytor might look relaxed, but he was ready to act at the slightest wrong move from Toby.

Toby clasped his hands behind his back and eyed them. "Has Legend ever told you about me?"

Pytor answered for them. "No, but I see he's told you about us."

"He has," Toby confirmed with a short nod. "I would consider you fools if you hadn't come after him. He's worth fighting for."

Yaro held Toby's stare. "He is." Yaro hoped Toby understood the unspoken threat behind his words. They would not allow anyone to stand in their way.

Toby didn't back down. "Legend has worked hard to make this party a success. Don't ruin it and prove him right that you care only about your wants."

"We have no intention of ruining your launch," Pytor said, sounding calm in the face of obvious confrontation.

"I'm not worried about the business." Toby's voice turned hard, matching his stare. "My brothers and I are already set for life. We didn't decide to start this company for ourselves. It's for people like Legend. People who give more of themselves than they take and have a talent for easing other people's lives, but who also aren't as fortunate as my family. Those people need protection from people like you—people who prey on the kindhearted."

Yaro's temper slipped. "We have made mistakes with Legend, but we have never preyed upon him. Pytor and I have done everything in our power to ensure he is never exploited again. We ensured he never has to work again. That knowledge is the only reason we are entertaining this conversation. We know he does not need this job. That means he cares for you in some way. His concern is your safety net right now, but it is a fine line you walk."

A malicious-looking smile tugged at Toby's lips, transforming him from the playful character he had shown Adrik earlier to an open adversary. "Don't be so sure I need that safety net. For now, you're guests in our home. The moment you step out of that role and hurt Legend, you will learn who that safety net is truly protecting." He flashed another feral smile. "Until then, enjoy your stay."

Pytor flashed Yaro an amused look as Toby closed the door behind him with a definite snap. "Cubs."

"It would seem they chose a fitting name." They shared a chuckle, but Yaro's humor quickly drained away. "There will be a room filled with ex-clients tonight, vying for Legend's attention. They mean nothing, but I wish to have him alone. He needs to hear our apology in private. I miss our baby. His eyes are sad again."

Pytor moved to the window and looked out. His tense expression screamed he was every bit as worried as Yaro that they didn't have enough time to say everything they needed to say. "We will find a way. Who are these people? This house is very nice for three young brothers."

Yaro stood and joined Pytor at the window. The view was amazing. A large pool glimmered below their window, but it wasn't a normal pool. It looked to be part of the natural surroundings with rock formations and streaming water. A gorgeous lake sat behind them with a boat tied to the dock. Yaro leaned to the left to see what else they had missed on their way in. A five-car garage sat to one side. A huge and expensive-looking black truck was parked on the stone driveway outside. Pytor and Yaro shared a glance. These boys were closer to Legend in age and obviously capable of taking care of him. Not that Legend needed them. Yaro and Pytor had ensured Legend never needed anyone. But it was fucking odd. The house was amazing. Yaro had noticed that right away, but it hadn't truly dawned on him that the triplets owned all of this until now. Yaro shook his head and let the mystery go. They had bigger issues—like how to get Legend alone.

Pytor kissed Yaro's nape. His eyes fell closed and his resolve doubled. He loved and missed Legend, but so did Pytor. Pytor had been Yaro's heart since he was six. He would do whatever it took to keep Pytor smiling. Knowing Pytor was hurting as much as Yaro from losing Legend was enough to make Yaro willing to sink to any low. They would get Legend alone and they would remind him how beautiful they were as a set. Yaro swore he could already taste Legend. He turned and captured Pytor's lips, absolutely convinced he could make Pytor taste Legend too. He couldn't wait until they held their angel again.

EIGHT

THE BALLROOM TURNED OUT LOOKING AMAZING. Toby, Tucker, and Tanner looked even better. Men hovered around them like flies, listening to their pitch. One day, they would be the biggest provider of renting a date, handyman, or simply someone to sit and keep an employer company. It was amazing how many people just wanted someone to talk to. Everything was going as planned. Legend would have patted himself on the back if he wasn't such a wreck.

Thankfully, he had his friend at his side. Adrik was adorable in his tuxedo. He kept pushing his glasses up and pulling at the hem of his jacket in a nervous gesture that tugged at Legend's heart.

Legend stuck to Adrik, making sure no one crowded his space. It was the least he could do for pulling Adrik so far out of his comfort zone so he wouldn't have to do this alone.

Legend's gaze slid to the edge of the room without his permission. Yaro and Pytor wore matching understated tuxedos, but Legend recognized the brand. They were insanely expensive and cut perfectly. Legend's mouth watered every time he looked their way. It was odd. By the way they had behaved earlier, Legend expected to be fending them off at every turn. The pair stuck to the fringes while keeping a close watch on Adrik. Legend hadn't decided how to feel. On one hand, he was relieved. If Legend knew nothing else, he knew he couldn't stand against their combined charm. On the other hand, his whole body ached from staying tensed the entire night. He loved them. It was a sickness. This was why he had left town. He couldn't be trusted to be near them. With them in the same room, Legend wanted nothing more than to throw good sense to the wind and beg them to keep him. He didn't understand why love had to be so hard.

"Look alive," Toby said, sailing by. "Henry Krill is headed your way."

"Fuck." Legend hadn't invited Henry. He also hadn't known he was there.

"Who's Henry?" Before the question fully died on Adrik's lips, Henry appeared.

"Legend."

Adrik automatically took a step closer to Legend, as if Henry's sudden appearance made him uncomfortable.

Legend wrapped his arm around Adrik's waist before acknowledging Henry. "Henry."

Henry's gaze moved Adrik's way. He smiled kindly before focusing on Legend once more. "May I have a moment of your time?"

"I suppose." Even as he agreed, he didn't move. Whatever Henry had to say, he could say there. Legend was finished accommodating people.

Henry shifted uncomfortably and cleared his throat. "All right. I need you to accept my apology."

"Was that it?"

A small smile touched Henry's lips at Legend's sassy tone. "I'm sorry. Sometimes, my mind is my worst enemy, but I never meant to hurt you."

Legend dipped his chin. "Apology accepted."

Henry's gaze slipped Adrik's way before sliding back to Legend. He looked like the last thing he wanted to do was talk in front of an audience, but Legend didn't offer him privacy. "I need to know. Did you intend to accept my proposal before I ruined everything?"

"Which one?" Honestly, Legend didn't care if the man meant his marriage proposal or the one to be his whore. He was simply enjoying Henry's discomfort. Legend wasn't really angry with him, but Henry had hurt his feelings. Maybe being put on the spot would make him think twice next time.

Henry visibly straightened his spine, obviously determined. "My marriage proposal."

Legend hesitated. Part of him had really believed Henry meant his offer. That small belief wanted him to lash out. In the end, he decided honesty was always best. "Yes."

Henry deflated, looking lost. "Is there anything I can do or say that will convince you to take another chance on me?"

"No," Adrik said, practically shouting, as if he couldn't contain himself a second longer. Henry's gaze snapped to Adrik. Adrik's jaw was hard. He looked ready to do battle on Legend's behalf. Before Henry could say a word or Adrik could tear into him, Tanner appeared.

He snagged Henry's waist. "Let's dance."

"I don't want to dance." Henry sounded outraged.

"Well, you're in for a real treat, then, because I don't either," Tanner said, sounding firm as he swept Henry away.

"Quick. Make a run for it before he gets away from what's his name," Adrik said, pushing Legend toward the stairs.

Legend automatically looked around, searching for Pytor and Yaro. They were nowhere to be seen. A shot of disappointment blasted Legend in the chest as he jogged up the stairs with Adrik shoving him along. He had lost his chance. Soon they would be gone. There would be no more dancing while people watched with envy. No more dinners where Pytor told him what he would eat. Legend smiled at the memory. Goddamn. He rubbed his chest. Legend missed his sexy, overbearing daddies.

Once they were up the stairs and safe from Henry finding them, Adrik started laughing. It was loud and filled with happiness. Legend couldn't help but smile at the sound. Adrik covered his mouth trying to stifle the sound. His eyes swam with humor. He fanned his face.

"Oh my god. I just yelled at that guy."

Legend chuckled at Adrik's obvious horror. "Yep. You were fierce and amazing."

Adrik punched Legend in the arm without warning. "You planned to marry that guy. What the hell? You're in love with Pytor and Yaro. You don't marry someone if you don't love them."

"He seemed the safe choice." Legend shrugged. "Not that it matters now."

Adrik shook his head and headed for his room. "I'm going to change. I'm uncomfortable as hell. You need to go talk things out with Yaro and Pytor before anyone else tries stealing you. You're too popular for your own good." He paused and focused on Legend. "I imagine it's harder to be beautiful than people realize."

Legend shook his head. Adrik was so blind. "Angel, you're one of the sexiest men I have ever met. So, if anyone would know, it's you."

Adrik rolled his eyes and opened his bedroom door. "I love you. Pytor and Yaro are waiting in your room. Promise me you'll try."

"I love you too."

"Promise me," Adrik repeated, refusing to let it go.

Legend drew an X on his chest. "Cross my heart."

"You say the weirdest shit," Adrik said, closing the door in his face.

Legend snorted into the empty hallway. He always forgot Adrik hadn't been a child. A wave of sadness overcame him. He wondered if Yaro and Pytor had gotten to be children. Legend couldn't fathom his men enduring anything like Adrik had. It was hard enough knowing his friend had suffered. He couldn't deal with knowing Pytor and Yaro had been abused.

Legend took a deep breath and moved to his bedroom door. He flattened his hand on the wood. They were on the other side. Legend could practically feel them waiting. He pressed his forehead to the cool surface and prayed for strength as he turned the knob. The first sight of them tightened Legend's chest. They sat side by side on the foot of Legend's bed. With their jackets missing and their sleeves rolled up their elbows, Pytor and Yaro looked ready to wait all night. They also looked sad. Legend's throat swelled at the thought.

"You two take my breath away every time I see you. Every single time," Legend said as he closed the door behind him. He concentrated on peeling off his jacket to keep his eyes from eating them alive. Legend undid his bow tie. "I try chastising myself when you're not around, because you're not really free to feel the same, but then I see you both again and I'm an idiot all over again. It's not fair, to be honest." With nothing left to distract him, Legend crossed his arms and faced them. "Say what you came to say."

"We're not sorry," Yaro said, surprising a chuckle from Legend.

"I know." They weren't built like that, but he had never expected them to admit it.

"At least, not for everything," Pytor said, throwing in his two cents. "Since we met, you have always had a sadness behind every smile. Sometimes, we made it go away and we're not sorry about that."

Legend's throat tightened. He didn't want to be their charity case. Legend didn't want to hear that he had been a project for them. He wanted them to love him, the way he had fallen in love with them. "I am." Even Legend heard the way his voice broke. "I'm sorry that I stepped between you two, especially now that I know you only let me in so you could fix me."

Pytor growled and scrubbed his hands over his face, as if Legend made him insane.

Yaro pulled a pained face. "We are not good at expressing ourselves. That is not what we meant." Yaro took a breath. His sexy wide shoulders heaved.

Legend couldn't look away. "I don't know how to put into words how we came to need you. That sneaked in. What Pytor tried to explain is, we wanted you to be with us always from the moment we met. Because of that, when we saw that you were hurting, instead of simply asking why and fixing whatever answer you gave, we took over and... well, I guess we just took over. That's what we are sorry for, but letting you in, we will never apologize for that."

They both looked so defeated, it tore at Legend's heart. They made it hard to fight, especially since Legend loved this gigantic pair of dumbasses. He cleared his throat, trying to speak around the pain of losing them. "It's not all on you two. I should've tried harder to make you both understand that I didn't feel equal in our relationship." Legend tapped his foot in his nervousness. His arms automatically tightened around himself. Losing them was slowly murdering him. They would never understand how much he loved them and how badly he wished he could be on the same level footing as them, but he wasn't.

"Why are you unhappy all the time?" Pytor asked, sounding heartbroken.

Yaro jumped in too. "We know we are late asking, but we are asking this time. What is it you need to be happy? What did we not give you?" Yaro looked like he knew the answer wasn't them.

A lump filled Legend's throat. The sadness was choking. He wanted to tell them that he was dying without them. That he was sad because they weren't his, but he knew what they meant. They wanted to know why being with them never took away all the pain. "It didn't have anything to do with you. My mom died. She was all I had." Legend's shoulders lifted and fell. Life was too heavy. Pytor and Yaro's expression shifted, as if they had been hit with the last thing they expected. He knew they thought it had been them. They had thought it was something they could fix. Legend kept talking. "It's weird when the only person you have to talk to is gone, and you don't even have anyone to tell that they're gone. Then I met you two less than a week later. Even though you both made me smile, I didn't feel like I had to, if that makes sense. I'm used to feeling like I always have to entertain everyone. That's my job and just ingrained in me, I guess, but not with you. I was stupid to fall in love with a married couple. Even as it was happening, I knew it was dumb, but you both made me feel like I belonged—like I had a home and a family. Then, you shut me out." Legend swallowed. The pain never stopped being as fresh as it was the moment he had felt the wall erect between them. "It's one thing to be alone in the world. That sucks. But being alone in the world while with someone is even worse. It's my fault. I know that. You've been together a long time. I was the intruder. But, for the record, I wanted us. I wanted what I wished we could be before I realized I would always be an outsider."

"You love us."

Legend bit back a tired sigh at Yaro's words. "Is that really your takeaway?"

"Why didn't you tell us about your mom?" Pytor asked as they both chose to ignore his question.

Legend shrugged. "I don't know. Maybe I didn't feel like I could. I already didn't feel like I was your equal. You two have money and each other. All I brought to the table was me. I didn't want to be any less worth keeping than I already felt like I was. Nobody likes being around someone pathetic and sad."

Yaro stood and closed the distance between them. "There is nothing you cannot say to us. You are a part of us. We want to help you carry everything, even your grief." He glanced Pytor's way and Pytor stood to hover over Legend too. They linked fingers before they each took one of Legend's hands. "We will be very truthful with you now too," Yaro said, sounding determined. His tone had Legend staring hard at him, waiting. Yaro took an audible breath. "We have been very hard on the inside for all our lives. To survive, there was no other choice. For many years, the only time we could be soft was when we were alone together. Since our old boss, the Conti, died, we have been free. But it is hard to let go of old habits. We lived on our toes for too many years, expecting beatings or worse. Many times, Conti threatened to strip away the fake lives he created for us, leaving us to either go to prison or be deported, or both. Any of those scenarios would have taken us away from each other. You are not allowed to be gay where we are from. We do not have a family other than each other. Not anymore. When we fell in love with you, we had every intention of you being a part of our tiny family, but we are not very good at it."

"You love me." Legend heard himself. He fully recognized he had been irritated over Yaro only coming away with that much from his speech. Now he had done the same. But really, he had heard every word. It was just that he never expected to have their love. Not really.

Pytor chuckled. It was deep and rumbling. Sexy.

"Idiot. Of course we love you. We would not have messed with you otherwise. As you have pointed out many times, we don't truly need anyone else. We are very happy together, but you captured both of us without our permission." Yaro nodded along as Pytor continued. "You are unique to us. Each time we spent time with you, you would smile and flirt, making us smile and flirt. When you left, we would look at each other and shake our heads. We did not know what was happening. You say you did not mean to love us. It was not our intention to love you either. Maybe we're not very good at it, but I still think this happened for a reason. I still think we were meant to be. We would like to try."

Yaro nodded. "I know we ask a lot when we failed you so much last time, but this is real. You are not our pet. We are just overbearing, because we are used to having to make hard choices, but we are also willing to do whatever it takes to be with you. If you want to stay here, we will visit as much as we can. If you wish to come home, you can put us in shock collars and pain train us to listen better."

A burst of laughter escaped Legend. He could picture them in collars.

Pytor smiled. It was sweet and took Legend's breath. "We are always listening, whether it seems like it or not. But it doesn't count unless you feel like you're heard. We love you. Tell us what you need to love us back again, because we are very sad without you."

Yaro nodded. "You were right. We didn't need you, yet you are completely necessary to us. You brought a light into our lives. One we didn't have before because our relationship started under such dark circumstances. You took that light away when you left. Our hearts are broken."

Legend was elated, devastated, and confused. He loved them and wanted to be with them, but he had been the same before. His chest ached. At some point, he had moved to hold their waists. They stood in a circle, inches apart, and sharing air. Legend was exhausted and didn't know what to do, but he couldn't pull away. He stared at his feet with his bottom lip held between his teeth. His men were warm, steady, and it hit Legend. They were his men and he could count on them. Legend had known they would show up eventually. Not once had he believed they were over for good. As much as he had known they needed some time apart to think, Legend had not doubted them.

"My house already sold." Legend didn't look at either man as he made the confession.

They didn't respond right away. Instead, they shifted closer until their temples touched his. Legend fought the urge to cry. These were his people. Pytor finally responded, sounding hesitant, as if he didn't want to make another misstep. "We hoped you might consider coming to live with us, but we understand if you can't."

Legend found himself stroking their backs. "I haven't slept much without you."

Yaro's lips found Legend's cheek. "We would keep you warm." His lips brushed Legend's skin with each word.

Pytor kissed the shell of his ear. "You will always be well rested... no matter how late we kept you up." The way he said "up" had Legend's dick twitching. Damn. They were the personification of desire.

"Come home," Yaro pled, kissing his way to the corner of Legend's mouth. "We will not make you sorry."

Legend's lips parted on a pant and Yaro took advantage. He captured Legend's bottom lip between his teeth. Legend could barely breathe. With his eyes closed and both men touching him and placing light kisses on his face and neck, Legend couldn't think straight. All he could do was feel. His shirttails were tugged from his pants. The buttons loosened on Legend's shirt until the two halves fell apart. Lips moved to his chest.

"Okay."

Both men froze.

Pytor tugged his hair, forcing his eyes open and his gaze to Pytor's. "Okay, what?"

"I'll come live with you."

Pytor's eyes fell closed in obvious relief. He visibly swallowed as if the news tightened his throat.

"I love you."

Yaro's confession had Legend's gaze jumping to his. Yaro was completely focused on Legend. He looked sincere.

"We both do," Pytor said, making Legend's heart skip a beat.

"I love you too." Legend looked between them, making sure they understood he meant both of them. "We'll make this work. I believe in us."

Yaro stripped while holding his gaze. "We believe in us too. You will always be proud to be together." As Yaro tossed his shirt aside, Legend's gaze skirted down Yaro's body. Long raised scars crisscrossed his sides. Legend knew from seeing them nude in the past, both men had similar scars across their backs. He had never felt free to ask what caused them. But those scars took on new meaning with Adrik and Yaro's claims about their pasts. No one would hurt them or steal the light from their lives again. Legend would do whatever it took. They were his. No one harmed them.

THERE WAS A LINGERING ACHE IN YARO'S CHEST from the fear of Legend's rejection. As they stripped nude, quietly accepting they would go to bed now as the set they were, Legend stared at him with a warrior's glint in his eyes. Yaro knew Legend would fight for them. He could feel it. They planned to be every bit as fierce in their battle to keep Legend. But at the moment, Yaro needed to feel Pytor's and Legend's bare skin against his. He needed the connection. Yaro wanted them so badly he didn't know where to start. This was why Pytor was almost always in charge. Yaro always wanted too many things that his brain froze, and he did nothing.

Legend cupped the back of Pytor's neck and crooked his finger at Yaro, beckoning him closer. "I've missed your tongues. They're mine. I want them."

A sexy, low chuckle rumbled from Pytor's chest. The sound made Yaro's cock jump as he leapt forward to give Legend his wish. He too had missed their kisses—the fight for air and dominance only three people could accomplish while kissing.

Legend drew them in. Lips brushed. Tongues curled. A firm hand stroked his cock. Yaro's entire body lit with stimulation. His nerve endings danced, anticipating more. "I want to be in the middle." The desperate plea burst from Yaro without his permission. He wanted them too badly to stay silent.

Legend stroked his cheek and traced his jaw. He looked understanding—like he would give Yaro the world. "I've missed you both so much. Tell me where you want me. Anything you need, it's yours."

Yaro glanced Pytor's way. Pytor looked equally ready to do whatever. His flushed cheeks and the way he kept kissing Legend's shoulders let Yaro know Pytor wouldn't last much longer without taking control. He was too turned on to show patience. It was now or never. "Get in bed. On your back."

Legend did as told while giving them one hell of a show. He made sure they saw him stroke his cock and flex his ass before settling down on his back. He linked his fingers behind his head, openly waiting.

Pytor and Yaro exchanged a look. It was like they

had a table of their favorite foods waiting. They made a silent vow to be thankful for every bite.

"I haven't really unpacked everything I brought, but I think there's a small tube of lube in a toiletry bag in the bathroom."

Pytor nodded. "I will get it." His sexy gaze moved over Yaro's face, setting Yaro's skin ablaze. "You will need it."

Oh god. He hoped. Even though he was a little nervous, Yaro wasn't backing down. Since falling for Legend, and realizing he wanted two men, Yaro hadn't stopped fantasizing about having both men inside him at once. Pytor had helped him practice by taking him and a dildo at the same time. Yaro knew it wouldn't be the same. He didn't care. As he crawled onto the bed with Legend and ran his tongue up Legend's length, Yaro vowed he wouldn't stop no matter what. Even if he decided he hated this and never did it again, Yaro needed the connection. He wanted their souls to touch.

Legend stroked every place he could reach. His whole body writhed like Legend couldn't contain his lust. Pytor reappeared with the small tube of lube. Without preamble, he leaned over the bed and coated Legend's cock.

"This is new for us." Pytor stroked his dick,

making it shine with lube. "I don't know how it will go."

Legend chuckled. The sound was ridiculously sexy. "Yaro will get his wish. Climb onboard, sexy," Legend said, waving his cock at Yaro. Yaro appreciated Legend keeping the mood light. He straddled Legend. Pytor joined them in bed. Legend's eyes flashed with heat. "You're both so fucking sexy."

Yaro practically vibrated with pride as Legend's cock filled his ass. He leaned forward and pressed his lips to Legend's chest. Otherwise, he didn't move. Yaro savored the sensation of being fully seated on Legend. Pytor toyed with Yaro's asshole, fingering him, and stretching. Everything felt too good. Yaro's cock leaked on Legend's stomach.

Pytor flattened his hand against the small of Yaro's back, holding him in place. "You are doing so good, sexy. Legend and I will make you beg for more."

"Yes," Legend hummed beneath him, sounding like a man on the edge. "You'll plead for us to fuck you like this all the time."

A whimper escaped him. Yaro couldn't hold it in. Legend and Pytor worked to make room for Pytor. Something much larger than Pytor's finger pushed inside him, working its way toward joining Legend's cock. Yaro bit Legend's chest.

Legend moaned. "That's it, baby. Use me. I want it."

Pytor slid the rest of the way in, and Yaro breathed through the intrusion. They didn't move. Instead, they gave Yaro a minute to adjust.

"Fuck, Yaro. I will not last long like this with both my men so intimate on my meat. You two will break me," Pytor said with a definite purr to his voice.

Yaro felt powerful—like he could do anything. "Fuck me." The plea slipped from Yaro with no input from his brain. He was a bundle of pure need.

Pytor took charge, setting the pace. He moved slow, ensuring Yaro didn't hurt, and neither cock slipped from his ass. Legend whimpered and moaned like the combination of Yaro's ass and Pytor's cock was driving him wild. With his erection trapped between Legend's and his bodies, Yaro barely had an ounce of sanity left. He was in sensory overload. His orgasm built. Pressure beat at his crown. Tiny sparks of pleasure pulled his brain in every direction. All Yaro could do was gasp and hold on. His every fiber was focused on explosion. He needed that release to match the ferocity of his feelings for these men. They were his. He would die for them. Kill for them. When they made it back home, Yaro swore he would do whatever it took to cling to this beautiful thing they were together. It had never mattered if anyone else understood. This was amazing. It was meant to be. A loud gasp tore from Yaro, hurting his throat as cum shot from his dick, filling the space between Legend's and his body.

"Jesus fucking Christ," Legend groaned, adding fuel to Yaro's orgasm. "Oh my god. You're sucking me dry. Fuck. Fuck." It was like Legend had been rendered senseless. His entire body spasmed beneath Yaro.

Pytor full-on growled—like a wild animal as he thrust against them. "So goddamn sexy. Mine. You're both mine."

Yaro clung to Legend and let them fill his ass. He was in heaven. Yaro had pleased his men. He was the reason they shook and were incoherent. That was him. He was so goddamn proud. For the rest of their days, he would keep these men happy. They were his, and he was theirs. The future looked beautiful.

THERE WASN'T A WORD IN ANY OF THE languages Pytor spoke to describe how Pytor felt watching his men sleep. He wouldn't fuck this up again. As much as he wanted to stay there and stare at Legend and Yaro until they woke and begged him to stop, he needed to check on Adrik. Pytor eased from the bed while holding his breath. They looked so peaceful. Pytor didn't want to wake them. Neither man stirred. Pytor released his pent-up breath and walked softly to the door. He eased it open and slipped out. As he gently closed the door behind him, another door opened down the hall. Henry stepped out—hair on end and shoes in hand, looking like he was running from the scene of a crime.

Pytor chuckled.

Henry's head snapped up. From the way his gaze shifted from side to side—like searching for an exit, Pytor wondered exactly whose room the man didn't want to be seen leaving.

Pytor couldn't let the opportunity pass. "Well, the only thing missing from this walk of shame is a broken heel and smeared lipstick." Even Pytor heard the heavy laughter in his voice. "Are you sneaking away from someone else you gave false promises of marriage?"

Henry's eyes narrowed. "Has no one ever told you that staff shouldn't see anything?"

Pytor snorted and turned away. "What an idiot," Pytor said more for himself than Henry. If the man possessed an ounce of sense, he would have stolen Legend out from underneath them and never looked back. No doubt, if he hadn't been such a pussy, Henry could have given Legend a good life, but Legend belonged to Yaro and him. They would never let him go. Henry meant nothing to Pytor.

Pytor tapped on Adrik's bedroom door. After a moment of shuffling on the other side, the door swung wide. Leo stood on the other side, wearing nothing but a sheet from the bed wrapped around his waist. It seemed Adrik hadn't made it through the night.

Leo scrubbed at his face. "Hey, man. What's up?"

"I was just checking on Adrik. Sorry to wake you."

Leo waved off his apology. "It's all good. I'm always grateful for the backup." His gaze skirted over Pytor, openly inspecting him. "You look better today. Did you get to talk to Legend?"

The smile tugging at his lips was out of his control. Pytor was over the moon at the moment.

"Yes. Everything is fine. He will be coming back with us. I'll let you know later when to be ready to leave. Legend might still wish to spend the rest of this weekend with his friends before going home. I'll keep you posted. Go back to bed before Adrik gets cold."

"Sounds good," Leo said, glancing behind him as if truly worried Adrik might be cold. "We'll be around."

Pytor nodded and turned to head back to his room. Henry stood with his shoulder leaned against the wall, openly waiting for Pytor's attention.

"So you've managed to win Legend."

"He isn't a game to win. Legend is a person with thoughts and feelings." Pytor took a step closer. "And, yes, those thoughts and feelings are mine, so if you ever think to try to trample them again, you won't get a chance to regret it next time."

To Pytor's surprise, Henry's mouth lifted in one corner. He straightened away from the wall. "That's oddly comforting." A sad smile passed over Henry's lips. He didn't quite meet Pytor's stare. "He's a good person. Sweet. People like him get eaten alive in this world without protection." He moved past Pytor toward the stairs without looking back. "I would know."

Pytor watched him go. He wished he didn't pity the guy, but Pytor did. Pytor knew what it was like to lose Legend. It was a nightmare he wouldn't wish on anyone.

With a final shake of his head, Pytor slipped back inside his room. Yaro and Legend were still sound asleep. There was no time like the present to start fixing all the ways he had gone wrong.

He slid beneath the covers and stroked Legend's jaw. Legend's gorgeous blue eyes opened and focused on Pytor. He lit with happiness.

"Good morning, sexy."

Pytor couldn't stop smiling. He truly owned the world. "I don't know this house. Do you want to help me make Yaro breakfast?"

A smile spread across Legend's lips, making Pytor wish he had been willing to relinquish a little control sooner. Legend's hand slid across Pytor's hip, pushing his shorts down. "Maybe I can convince you to stay here instead."

It wouldn't be hard. Pytor was onboard to be convinced to do whatever Legend wanted. "I'm listening."

A happy-sounding giggle filled the air, making Pytor smile as Legend disappeared beneath the covers. Pytor's chest filled with pride. Legend looked so damn happy this morning. They had done that. Legend shimmied down the bed, kissing Pytor's chest and stomach while divesting him of his shorts. Pytor sucked air as Legend kissed his cock. His gasps turned to moans as Legend set a pace to please. His mouth disappeared and Legend kept the same pace with his hand.

Yaro came awake with a start. A low moan escaped him, making Pytor realize where Legend's mouth had disappeared to. Pytor stared at Yaro's open lust as he rode Legend's hand. Legend switched between them, sucking and pumping. Pytor scooted closer, incapable of stopping. Legend's mouth felt too good. Yaro met his stare. He tilted his chin down in a silent gesture. They shared a wicked smile. As one, they moved, snagging Legend and flipping him around. They caught a glimpse of surprise before they were all about the dick.

Their tongues licked at Legend's erection while finding each other. They kissed and tongued Legend at the same time. Legend's motions turned frantic. He jacked at their cocks while sucking each one, as if he couldn't decide which one he wanted. Pytor's mind was split. He wanted Legend's cum and Yaro's tongue, but he also needed the orgasm Legend's mouth and hands promised. His hips rolled, openly seeking more. Legend didn't let up. Neither did Yaro nor Pytor. They worked hard at pleasing one another. Pytor's body tensed so hard he felt a tiny muscle pull in the bottom of his foot. His cock hit the back of Legend's throat. An orgasm ripped from him along with a cry. He sucked Legend's crown hard in his mindless pleasure. Legend's body stiffened. Cum filled Pytor's mouth. Yaro moved to share it with him. Together they licked Legend clean while Yaro whimpered through an orgasm. No doubt they had painted Legend's face in cum. Pytor smiled at the picture.

His throat swelled out of nowhere. He had to get his men home. Pytor wouldn't feel secure again until they were all back under his roof. "Please tell me you don't have a ton of stuff that needs to be moved before you can come back home." Pytor sounded desperate and needy to his own ears.

Legend released a tired-sounding laugh. "All my stuff, including my car, is in storage in California. All I have here is some clothes."

"Thank fucking god," Pytor breathed, collapsing into the mattress. Without thought, he stroked himself. These two men would probably kill him, but he had so many plans for them. "I love you both."

"Same," Yaro breathed, sounding half dead.

Legend pressed a hand to each of their stomachs. "I love you both too." He chuckled, sounding so happy that Pytor swore, even his heart smiled. "I hope you two intend to start a solid vitamin regimen because I plan to put your backs out."

Pytor snorted as he covered his eyes. He couldn't wait. His back and he were up to the challenge. Nothing sounded better at the moment.

NINE

In a bid to meet his men halfway, Legend had let the cancellation of his gym membership stand. Plus, he kind of loved the extra time with Yaro and Pytor while working out. He equally enjoyed the peaceful sound of the waterfalls at the indoor obstacle course. Living with Pytor and Yaro felt a lot like he had found a family. Things were night and day this time around. All three of them tried harder to compromise, and Legend had never been happier in his life, especially since he recognized this was the rest of his life. The three of them were forever. He also low-key loved sharing a home with Adrik. Sometimes, it was funny, because the place was so huge, Legend had yet to run into Zander or his husband Maverick. In fact, most of the time, it felt like Pytor, Yaro, and he were the only people who lived there. Other times, Adrik was underfoot like a roommate and Legend loved getting to have his friend around like that. He was at peace here.

Legend focused on putting his climbing gloves on as he cleared the doorway to the obstacle course. He stopped in his tracks as he caught sight of a shirtless blond man. The guy was beautiful. He was sleek with every muscle well-defined. His ice-blue eyes focused on Legend and didn't budge.

A smile stretched the guy's lips. "You must be Legend. I'm Zander," he said, stepping forward and extending his hand. He had never seen Zander Kapra up close.

Legend accepted his handshake. He had to admit Zander wasn't anything like he expected. For one thing, he would have thought the man running the west coast would be older. Zander was probably a few years younger than Pytor and Yaro. "It's nice to finally meet you."

"The feeling is mutual." Zander looked nice. Legend automatically felt at ease. Zander motioned toward the course behind him. "Since we're both here, would you care to race? It's always good to have some competition to keep you on your toes."

Legend nodded. "Sure. I'm always up for a challenge."

Zander chuckled—like he could already taste his win. Legend had no plans of being a pushover today. Zander moved to the closest wall and fired up the sound system. Loud metal music filled the air. It was odd how at ease he felt with Zander—like they were immediate friends.

"You know the trick to winning this course, right?" Zander yelled over the music.

"Of course," Legend said, suppressing a smile.

"What is it?" Zander asked the question like he was certain Legend didn't really know.

"Cheat." Legend shot past Zander without looking back. A loud laugh rang out behind him as he grabbed for the first handhold. Between his huge head start and using a risky short cut, bypassing two metal rings between hills, Legend still managed to only beat Zander by a much shorter length than he liked. By the time they stood at the top of the stone structure, they were both breathing heavy. Their gazes met, and they both burst out laughing. They were lucky they hadn't broken their necks. Nothing good could come of the two of them being left alone, since they were both obviously too competitive.

Loud clapping sounded below them. Pytor and

Yaro stood side by side, staring up at them. "Good job, sexy."

Yaro nodded his agreement to Pytor's praise. "Zander is rarely beaten. He is usually a much bigger cheat."

Legend fought a blush. Their pride in him was always the biggest stroke to his ego. Zander climbed down. Legend followed. He didn't hesitate to accept each man's kiss. Legend never got tired of their affection.

Once they were all on the same level, Zander turned down the music a hair. "It's good to see your lazy asses finally made it. Do you two have plans to show us how it's done?"

Pytor made a sexy humming noise that had Legend pressing a hand to his stomach, trying to squelch the instant hunger. "We are up for a leisurely climb but keeping up with this young pup has these two old, lazy asses—as you say—too tired to race."

Legend didn't win against his blush this time. Zander didn't try hiding his laughter at Legend's open embarrassment. Yaro, Pytor, and Zander had known each other their whole lives. Nothing was off the table with them, including Legend wearing them out in bed, it seemed.

Zander swiped at his eyes. "I guess it's up to us then, Legend. This time, I say we make it a little more interesting. How about a wager?"

"Um." Legend shifted from one foot to the other. "What sort of wager?" Legend didn't know how much Zander was worth, but he imagined it was easily in the billions, and Legend couldn't match that.

A wicked light entered Zander's eyes. "Nothing too huge. If you win, I'll let you steal Pytor and Yaro away for two weeks. I'll even throw in an all-expense paid trip to wherever you choose for the three of you."

Legend nodded. He kind of liked that. "And if you win?"

The moment the question left his lips, Legend swore he felt an invisible trap close by Zander's expression alone. "You have to agree to a plan Pytor, Yaro, and I have worked out for your future."

Without his permission, Legend's brows snapped together. He didn't care for plotting behind his back. "What plan?"

Zander didn't look the least bit bothered by Legend's irritation. "Legally speaking, you can't marry them, but we're not bothered a lot by the law here. To be honest, most of the people living under this roof aren't even in this country legally. Our identities aren't real, but they would hold up under the harshest of scrutiny. So there's nothing saying we couldn't hold a wedding ceremony, change your last name, and ensure you are a legally entitled joint partner in their lives. If I win, you have to agree to that plan."

Shock had Legend's gaze sliding Yaro and Pytor's way. They both appeared hopeful. A nervous-looking smile passed over Yaro's lips. "It would be a marriage in our hearts, and we would always honor it as such."

Legend couldn't think. Since he had come back from Texas with the pair three months earlier, he had convinced himself that he could live with never being anyone's husband. That being loved by them was more important than any title. This offer felt real. His eyes stung. He knew Pytor and Yaro. They had strong characters. This would be a real marriage to them, no matter what the law said.

He focused on Zander. "I accept your terms." Even to Legend's ears, it sounded like he had been gargling gravel.

With a sharp nod, Zander held out his hand. "Then we'll shake on it. No cheating this time. Whoever wins, the other will know it was a fair loss."

Legend swallowed as he shook Zander's hand. It would be a fair match. He couldn't look Pytor and Yaro's way. Legend didn't want them to see his heart. Instead, he tightened his climbing gloves while Zander set the countdown rules. The countdown began. Legend focused on the course ahead of him. It was a huge setup with rock formations reaching to nearly the top of the forty-five-foot ceiling. A waterfall split the rock and metal rings crossed from one side to the other. It wasn't completely safe to be racing, but they were men. They turned everything into a competition.

A horn blew through the sound system, signaling the start. Zander shot forward, flying toward the first set of handholds. Legend turned in the opposite direction, heading for Pytor and Yaro. He wouldn't lose for just anyone, but this didn't feel like a loss. Their expressions made his decision worthwhile. They looked like he handed them a bag filled with money—moved, speechless, and choked with emotion. They held hands and opened their arms to him. Legend walked into their hold, completing the perfect circle they made. He would love, honor, and cherish them for as long as they lived. Just as Legend didn't doubt for a moment, they would do the same, guarding his heart for the rest of their days. It was a beautiful future and Legend couldn't wait.

Toby, Tanner, and Tucker are the beginning of a new series, Cubs for Rent. Tanner's book will be first, First Loser.

ABOUT THE AUTHOR

Charity Parkerson is an award winning and multi-published author with several companies. Born with no filter from her brain to her mouth, she decided to take this odd quirk and insert it in her characters.

*Eight-time Readers' Favorite Award Winner

*2015 Passionate Plume Award Finalist

*2013 Reviewers' Choice Award Winner

*2012 ARRA Finalist for Favorite Paranormal Romance

*Five-time winner of The Mistress of the Darkpath

Connect with her online:

--Join my street team: facebook.com/TeamCharityParkerson

--Website: charityparkerson.com

--Facebook: facebook.com/authorCharityParkerson

facebook.com/TheMenofSin

--Twitter: twitter.com/CharityParkerso